Glistening Sunsets

A Mount Desert Island Series

Katie Winters

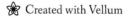 Created with Vellum

Chapter One

Twenty-Five Years Ago

Joseph Keating wasn't exactly pleased with his twenty-one-year-old daughter Brittany's decision to spend the summer in Boston. To him, a Bar Harbor "born-and-raised" who'd never traveled much of anywhere, Boston was half the distance to the moon away, and the urgency reflected in his eyes spoke of his fear that Brittany would never come back. Brittany tried her darnedest to console him but found soon that her words weren't enough. It was a father's duty to worry, and it was a child's duty to grow up. Those were the facts.

"You've always had a wild streak," her father finally said, disgruntled as he watched her slip her suitcase into the back of her best friend Mary's clunky second-hand car. "I've always known the day would come when I had to say goodbye."

"Dad, you're so dramatic," Brittany teased, falling into the familiar warmth of his bear hug. "It's only two months, and it's not enough time for me to develop a Boston accent."

Truth be told, Brittany's heart lifted with the volatility of freedom as Mary pressed her foot on the gas. Together, they raced out of that tiny town on the coast of Maine, away from the Keating Inn and Acadia Eatery, away from her responsibilities at the family-run inn, away from wiping tables and vacuuming under beds and from wearing that ridiculous maid's uniform.

"When will you tell your dad that you don't want to take over the Keating Inn when you're older?" Mary asked as they made their way further south.

"The man's delusional if he thinks I just want to pick up where he left off. The inn was him and my Uncle Adam's dream, not mine."

"But what do you want to do?"

June sunlight caught the tops of barns as they whipped past, careening toward a summer they would never forget.

"One thing I've adored about the Keating Inn." Brittany began, "Is picking out some of the furnishings for the rooms. Dad let me take over that portion of the business a few years back, and I researched antiques and vintage furnishings until my head spun. And now, I have a firm grasp of what to look for in historical pieces and how much they're worth."

Brittany let her head drift back against the headrest as her thoughts spun toward this impossible dream.

"I don't know if I'll ever have the money to put together a space for a little antique shop," Brittany breathed. "But I can't imagine a better idea than building a business from my deep-rooted passion."

* * *

Brittany and Mary had a two-month sublease in an apartment in East Boston. They'd been hired to work at a popular shoreline restaurant, which always looked for extra staff members during the heavier tourist season. Over those first few days, Brittany was delirious with all the new sights and sounds as she learned the ropes at the restaurant (along with who to joke with and who to avoid and who was willing to go out dancing afterward) and how to dig into the Boston scene. After twenty-one years in Bar Harbor, her heart and mind were more than ready for the renewed energy of a brand-new world.

It was this bright-eyed optimism that opened her heart to love.

Conner Radley was a handsome twenty-four-year-old fisherman who'd been born and raised in Boston and hired at his father's lobster fisherman company. Because of the nature of his job, his muscles were curved, thick, and refined, and his skin glowed with a healthy tan. When he first offered to buy Brittany a drink at a little seaside bar after Brittany's shift at the restaurant, Brittany's knees knocked together fearfully.

"I felt it— the thing they always say you'll feel when you meet the one," Brittany explained to Mary later that night after she returned home, bleary-eyed from one too many beers.

"All right, honey. Just don't get carried away," Mary teased her.

"I swear, Mary. This is different. When he looks at me, I can see our entire future and picture our babies."

"Your dad will kill you if you stay in Boston forever." Mary grabbed a large bag of potato chips, yanked it open, and placed a delicate chip on her tongue.

"Who knows..." Brittany returned, throwing her hand into the bag. She was a ferociously hungry, tipsy twenty-one-year-old girl with too much on her mind, and chips hadn't yet begun to cling to her hips. "Maybe he'll love me so much that he'll come with me back to Bar Harbor. Or maybe... he'll never call me at all."

"Either story is currently possible," Mary pointed out.

"Guess we'll just have to wait and see how everything plays out."

Even with all the imagination in the world, Brittany couldn't have written out the beauty of her and Conner's love story. What began at that seaside bar flourished into long nights of whispered words, kisses beneath the moonlight, and late mornings of sleeping in (often resulting in Conner getting into wicked trouble with his father for missing his lobster fishing shift).

When the time came for Brittany to return to Bar Harbor, she spent all night weeping alongside a sleeping Conner, wishing for a different world. The restaurant didn't have any shifts left for the extra girls they'd hired over the summer, and if she was brutally honest with herself, she ached with homesickness. Mary already had her bags packed, ready to flee back to their Bar Harbor coast. Brittany knew that her love would remain here— toiling until it died altogether.

"Come with me." She whispered the words through the grey light of the morning, mere hours before Mary expected her back at their apartment for a final clean-up and check-out. "I don't know if you know this, but there are lobsters in Bar Harbor, and in fact, it's one of the things we're most known for."

It was like pressing fast-forward on life.

Within the next month, Conner Radley's father suited him up with a job with a friend-of-a-friend in Bar Harbor's lobster fishing ring. Conner moved into a studio apartment in downtown Bar Harbor, one with a mattress still on the ground and a bunch of boxes stacked in the corner. What did Brittany care about what his place looked like? She was head-over-heels for this man, and he'd decided to abandon his life altogether and build one there, with her.

There was just one problem with all of this.

Brittany hadn't yet gotten up the courage to introduce

Conner Radley to her father, the at-times-difficult Joseph Keating. Since Brittany's arrival back to Bar Harbor, her father had pushed her deeper into the Keating Inn, even as her simmering hatred for a career in hospitality grew. Her father also tried to have professional meetings with her about the future of the inn, ones that she often daydreamed through or flat-out skipped.

In Mid-October, as violent purple clouds descended over Bar Harbor, Conner surprised Brittany outside the Keating Inn at the end of her shift. She rushed to leap into the front of his truck and press her lips against his, shivering with longing. But instead of driving them immediately back to his place, Conner said he had a "surprise" for her, one that couldn't wait.

On the southern-most tip of downtown's Main Street sat the law offices of Goggins & Stanley. The same two persnickety and old-fashioned lawyers had resided in that historic building, making fat stacks of cash year after year, since Brittany could remember.

"What the heck are we doing here, Conner?"

Conner stopped the engine and wiggled his eyebrows. "You know I deliver lobsters exclusively to Goggins' and Stanley's wives."

"I didn't. But what's that got to do with—"

Conner cut her words off. "The wives are forcing them to retire this fall," he informed her simply. "Mrs. Goggins wants to move to Florida, and Mrs. Stanley wants to spend more time with the grandchildren."

"And?"

"Come on, Brittany." Conner wrapped his strong hands around the base of her head and gazed into her eyes lovingly. "This building was built in the late 1800s during the whaling boom. It has more cultural significance than even the courthouse. And by the beginning of December, it'll be empty, and it will be ready for a brand-new business. And the way Mrs.

Goggins and Mrs. Stanley talked about it... They would be very interested in hearing your plan for the place."

Brittany's lips parted in surprise. Never in all her days had someone gone so far out of their way for her and her silly little dream.

"They would, of course, maintain ownership over the building," Conner continued, filling in the blanks. "But they want a local business person to take over. And the way Mrs. Goggins talks..."

"She was always more gossipy than Mrs. Stanley," Brittany quipped.

"The fact that their husbands were the go-to lawyers in town means that several people have turned their backs on them. One person would use Goggins to sue a friend; that friend would use Stanley to sue the guy back... It turned into a mess that left them with very few friends."

"But plenty of money," Brittany added.

Conner's hands wrapped tenderly around hers as he blinked his large, hopeful eyes. "Tell me you'll think it over."

"I have to talk to my father," Brittany told him simply, her shoulders falling forward. "He has this image of us working at the Keating Inn, side-by-side."

"All you've done is complain about that old place since I met you," Conner said with a laugh. "Just promise me you'll get up the nerve to talk to him about it. You owe it to yourself. And you owe it to our future."

The conversation with Joseph Keating didn't exactly go "well," per se. Her father's eyes avoided Brittany's as she outlined her business plan and strategy for paying off the loan she required to pay the initial rent and fill the building with antiques. She'd never lived anywhere but the Keating House on the Keating property (besides Boston for two months), she'd saved up most of her Keating Inn pay checks and tips. Still, it wasn't enough for a young woman of twenty-one to open up an antique shop. Not even with all the talent in the world.

Joseph Keating's parting words were simply: "Let me think about it." And then, he added, "I guess it's about time I met that boyfriend of yours. Why don't you have him over for dinner?"

Two weeks later, only minutes before Conner arrived to meet Joseph Keating for the first time, Joe gave his daughter a bank slip which read that he'd deposited a twenty-five-thou-sand-dollar loan into her account. Brittany gaped at the number, one with far more zeros than she'd ever seen in her life, and thanked her father with stuttered words and many tears.

"Why did you change your mind?" Brittany asked him after their hug broke.

"I recognized me and your Uncle Adam in your eyes," her father told her. "I realized this meant just as much, if not more than the Keating Inn ever did to us. I couldn't stand in the way of that. Not when I knew I could help."

Brittany stood in the Keating House foyer watching as the love of her life and her father locked eyes and shook hands, performing the dramatic ritual of men. Conner had brought a half-decent bottle of wine and a bouquet of flowers, which he handed to Brittany tenderly. Still, a darkness unfurled from the back alleys of Joseph Keating's eyes. From the moment they met, it seemed clear that Joe didn't trust Conner whatsoever. It was as though he smelled something on him, a sort of sour flavoring that Brittany didn't catch.

Ever the optimist, Brittany pushed them through dinner with bright conversation, speaking excitedly with her hands, so much so that she nearly toppled a glass of wine. They ate salmon that was seasoned with lemon, mashed potatoes and broccoli, and all the while, Joseph continued to gape at Conner with a mix of distrust and disbelief. By contrast, Conner was on his best behavior, asking all the appropriate questions, performing the act of "good boyfriend meeting the father for the first time."

To distract her father, Brittany told Conner with enthusiasm about moving forward with the deal for the Main Street building. "I already have a plan drawn up for that main room," she stated. "And I've researched a number of local antique auctions to get myself started. Maybe you two can come with me? Help me lift some of the heavier furniture?"

Joseph Keating's smile waned. Conner arched an eyebrow as he forked a white wad of mashed potatoes across his tongue.

"I'm sure one of us could help you out, Brittany," Joe told her. "We'll make it work."

"I'm happy to do it," Conner returned, his tone sharp.

The men puffed out their chests almost menacingly. Brittany had never sensed this "territorial" nature in Conner before. She wanted to point out how silly he was acting, that these weren't the regency times— that she had no dowry and no real prospects to trade over to the interested marital party.

The three of them made their way through the rest of dinner. Joe half-mentioned something about dessert, but Brittany jumped at the chance to excuse herself from dessert. "I'm not eating sugar right now," she announced.

Joe looked relieved. Conner jumped to his feet and headed for the bathroom, leaving Brittany and her father in a tunnel of tension. Brittany twiddled her thumbs as the clock on the wall performed its sixty-second dance.

"Are you sure about this, Brittany?" Her father suddenly asked it, point-blank.

"Am I sure about what?"

"About..." Joe cast his eyes toward the gloomy hallway where Conner had disappeared.

"Conner and I are in love," Brittany hissed. "You were always so resistant to anyone I brought home. Boyfriends or friends or even study partners for that matter."

"That's not true."

"It is," Brittany told him firmly. "I need you to give Conner a chance. He moved here for me, and he will be around a long, long time."

The bathroom door shrieked, and, a moment later, Conner appeared in the foyer, reaching for their coats.

"Are you ready to hit the road?" Brittany called.

The color drained from Joe's cheeks. He stood and followed Brittany like a lost dog, all the way to the foyer. Brittany pulled the zipper of her coat to her chin and thanked her father for dinner and all of his help.

"I'll be back tomorrow," she told him, indicating, with a slight hesitation, that she'd made her choice. Probably, she and Conner would soon have enough set-aside to get a one-bedroom apartment of their own. She knew everything would work out.

And she hoped that Joe and Conner would someday find common ground.

Conner and Brittany drove back downtown to meet up with Brittany's friends in one of the local bars. Since his arrival, Conner's charm and good looks had placed him within the folds of Brittany's social life. He joked around with Brittany's guy friends and was protective and warm with Brittany around her girlfriends. Not one of them had pulled Brittany aside to say, "Are you sure?" In fact, more than one of Brittany's girlfriends had said, "Should I go to Boston to get my own Conner?"

Conner stopped the engine outside the bar and blinked through the darkness before them. The music filtered out through the frame of the building. Brittany began to ask if he was all right, but before she could finish the sentence, he lifted a hand and smashed it against the side of the steering wheel so that the truck quaked beneath them.

Brittany had never seen Conner so violent. She placed her

hand over her mouth to suppress her harsh squeal of surprise. When she blinked over at Conner, she found his face blood red.

"What the hell is wrong with that guy?" Conner demanded, speaking still toward the front glass of the truck.

Brittany's heart pumped with sorrow. Slowly, she lifted a hand toward Conner's, her fingers quivering with surprise. She wanted to tell him it would get better; she wanted to tell him this was only the beginning of the rest of their beautiful lives together. She wanted to tell him that Joseph Keating could be difficult but was almost always worth it.

But instead, Conner whipped his face toward her, his eyes as hungry as a wolf's. "You want to tell me it'll all be okay? Is that what you want to say?"

Conner had never used such a harsh, sarcastic tone with her. She yanked her head back as shock shivered in her stomach.

"Conner..."

"No," Conner told her firmly. "Don't. The way you and your father looked at me in there, it was like I was being picked apart for everything I stand for. No, I don't come from money. My father was only a fisherman, and I'm the same, nothing more than a fisherman."

"Conner, you know I don't care about that," Brittany told him.

"You? Growing up in that big house on the hill? You care about that much more than you know," he told her. "And you're lying to yourself if you don't see it."

"Conner, I love you, and I want to build a life with you. I..."

"I don't even know if it was worth it," Conner spat. "Coming all the way to this bottom-of-the-barrel town. You don't even know the kind of women I could have had, and I could have had anyone I pleased. And I came here, and I came here for you."

Brittany kicked out into the dark chill and hustled, bleary-eyed, for the back door of the bar. She ran inside, shivering, on the hunt for a friend, anyone to curl against as she shook against his frantic and hurtful words. She saw her friends in the corner, in the midst of a comical uproarious laugh. They looked like they belonged in a beer commercial.

But before she could reach them, a warm hand wrapped around her wrist, stopping her in her tracks. When she turned back, her eyes found the glorious love reflected back in Conner's eyes. The monster from the truck was no more. Her lip quivered as she dropped against him, allowing herself to be wrapped up in a hug.

"Why are you crying?" he whispered into her ear as she shook against him. "We're going to work this out, Brittany. I love you. I love you more than I ever thought was possible to love anyone. I'm scared, that's all."

Chapter Two

Last Autumn

"How do you talk about a man's life after it's over?" Brittany Keating Radley stood at the pulpit at the downtown Bar Harbor funeral home, her heart torn in two and her eyes still, miraculously dry. It was as though her body dared her not to show the significance of its trauma until after everyone went home and left her in peace. Off to the right of the front row, her daughter, Valerie, wept softly, dotting a Kleenex against the corner of her left eye, which was already stained black from her affection for too much eyeliner. Her brother, Thomas, sat on the other side of Conner, whose muscular arms curved around his chest, latched tight. Thomas was the spitting image of his father at that age, all dark hair and intelligent eyes and broad shoulders. Conner looked like he had somewhere else to be that day.

"When Dad first told me he was dying," Brittany continued after a brief hiatus, "I wanted to call his bluff. Joseph Keating wasn't the kind of man who wanted to leave any party early.

Whether it was your BBQ, your child's birthday, or your retirement party, Joseph Keating usually arrived with a bag of ice, extra food, and a helping hand. He was normally in the kitchen cleaning up long after everyone else left for the night— up to his elbows in soap suds, talking up a storm to whoever would listen. That was my Daddy."

Uh oh. The first of what would be many tears fell from the corners of her eyes. Brittany swiped them away and pushed herself through the remainder of her speech, which she'd rewritten five times the previous night. When Conner had asked if she wanted someone to edit it, she resisted, whipping the paper out between his hands. What could Conner Radley possibly know about Joseph Keating that she didn't? And hadn't the two men spent the previous twenty years at-odds with each other, barking out insults at the occasional family function when they couldn't all-out avoid one another?

After the ceremony, Brittany, Valerie, and Thomas stood near the casket to greet mourners and thank them for their attendance. Those invited were told to head to Brittany's place for the wake. She and Valerie had set aside over one-hundred tiny turkey sandwiches, spinach and artichoke dip, plenty of finger foods, and a large collection of red wine.

Mid-way through the line, Brittany's cousins, Nicole and Heather Harvey appeared. Nicole's face was blotchy, her eyes downcast with sorrow. Over the previous two years or so, Nicole had latched onto Joseph Keating like a lost puppy. She'd followed him around the Keating Inn and Acadia Eatery, asking him questions about the hospitality business, and often helping out in the kitchen as she cooked up vibrant and inventive recipes, ones she created herself.

"That Nicole is really something!" Joe had said more than once.

"He was so grateful you came to Bar Harbor," Brittany whispered into Nicole's ear now, as Nicole fell against her with a shivering hug. "He needed someone to fall in love with the Keating Inn the way he and Adam had. I never managed to, and I think it was one of his greatest sorrows."

"He loved you and was ridiculously proud of you," Nicole told her firmly. "Your antique shop was always his number one thing to brag about."

"He was so resistant at first," Brittany explained, swiping away new tears that rolled down her cheeks. "But he was instrumental in getting it all started. I'll never forget that he set aside his pride for me."

"Because he loved you," Nicole said. "And if there's anyone who knew how to love and love well... it was Uncle Joe."

Brittany greeted the hollowed-out Heather, who'd only just arrived at Bar Harbor for the first time. Heather's husband, Max, had recently died in a terrible accident out on the ocean. In the midst of a horrendous depression she couldn't shake, she'd come to Bar Harbor for answers about the Harvey sisters' past— a past that had always been Brittany's only reality.

In fact, having cousins for the first time had been something of a whirlwind. Brittany prayed they would stick around, lured in by the beauty of the sleepy little town on the coast, rather than return to their "real" homes in Portland. But she knew there was no controlling what anyone did. You just had to take the here and now and be grateful for it.

Perhaps as Joseph Keating's final joke to his daughter, Brittany was on full-scale hospitality duty at the wake. She was reminded of her long-ago days at the Keating Inn and Acadia Eatery, anticipating everyone's needs, cleaning up little messes, and finding empathy and goodwill in even the most banal conversations. It was only when she stalled at the kitchen counter and her knees knocked together that she remembered the depth of her fatigue.

"How are you holding up, Mom?" Valerie appeared beside her with a stack of plates and a bundle of dirty forks in her hand.

"Oh, honey. Thank you for picking those up." Brittany grabbed the stack and began to shuffle them into the dishwasher. "Have you seen your father?"

"I saw him in the backyard a little while ago," Valerie said testily. "Thomas asked him if he was planning on coming in."

Brittany dabbed the pad of her hand against the top of her forehead. She didn't have time to feel the devastation of her husband's lack of care for her father's death. In truth, Conner had hardly sniffed at Joe's illness; he'd hardly visited in the hospital when he'd been on the dramatic decline; he'd hardly held Brittany while she cried.

"Are you really happy, Brittany?" These were the words her father had whispered to her several months before, during a particularly heinous health spell that had latched him to a hospital bed for more than two weeks.

Brittany's voice had scratched with doubt. She'd wanted to ask him if happiness was a necessity or if it mattered at all. She'd wanted to say that her children were well-fed and intelligent and empathetic, that they had all the mechanisms to be incredible future people in the world.

Instead, she'd said, "I don't know. I think so."

The words had simmered with self-doubt.

"I've said this to you before," her father had whispered then, hardly able to get the words out. "But you can do whatever you need to do. You're a survivor. And if that means..."

Brittany had cut him off after that. The violence of hearing the words "leave him" only seemed to darken the bruise that had seemed, continually, to grow harsher over the previous twenty-some years. Brittany had noticed Conner's "true" self that very first evening with her father. And since then, Conner hadn't been too shy to let his true personality fly free. Cruelty lined many of their conversations, and his actions always seemed manipulative, especially those that were spontaneously kind.

Joseph Keating had taken one look at Conner and had known precisely what kind of man he was.

And Brittany had always been just a little too proud to admit how wrong she'd been.

That, and she'd loved him. God, she'd loved him. There had been a strange push-pull dynamic within their relationship. His kindness gave her fuel to keep going; when he reeled back, growing cold again, she fought tooth and nail to give him whatever he needed to smile again.

After over two decades, a flourishing business, and now, a father's funeral, Brittany felt herself nearing the end of her rope.

A few minutes later, as Brittany whipped out of the kitchen again to inspect the food table and greet several other Bar Harbor residents, Conner popped back inside from the backyard. On cue, he flashed that all-American smile at the nearest victim, who greeted him warmly and smacked him on the back.

"I'm just so sorry for your loss," the man said.

"It's been hard on us," Conner returned. "Joe was just such a great guy."

"It must have been a real pleasure, being his son-in-law."

"One of the greatest honors," Conner told him.

A shiver raced down Brittany's spine. Pausing at the corner table, she poured herself an extra-large serving of Cabernet Sauvignon, closed her eyes, and sucked down a quarter of it. She then turned with a flash on her back heel, slammed her shoulder into the nearest person, and threw half of the wine across his chest.

It was Conner. Of course, she'd done this to Conner. When it came to luck, she had none.

"Oh no!" Family and friends gasped around them. Someone rushed off to grab a towel.

Conner's face was a funny thing to read. Any other onlooker might have said that instantly. Conner's smile made everyone know that it was fine, that if anything, a spill at a funeral was something to laugh at. But Brittany caught the fire behind his pupils, proof that someday, and someday soon, Conner would make her pay for this. In his mind, she'd just embarrassed both herself and him, as he was her husband and therefore an extension of her. After twenty-four years together, she knew how his mind worked.

"Come on, Conner," Brittany whispered as coaxingly as possible. "Let's go to the kitchen and clean this up."

Conner wrapped his hand around hers, looking like the perfect picture of a husband. They then headed for the kitchen as Conner nodded down toward his shirt, making jokes. "She's a clumsy one. Don't know what to do with her some days."

Once in the kitchen, Conner unbuttoned his shirt as all the color drained from his cheeks. He then scrunched the shirt into a tight ball and flung it into the sink, where it toiled against a number of dirty dishes. If he hadn't been the most terrifying creature in Brittany's life, a part of her might have found this scene attractive— a powerful, handsome man in his late forties with salt-and-pepper hair and toned muscles, wearing only an undershirt.

"You know that a number of my clients are out there," he breathed. "You know that if I come off like some kind of fool..."

"Conner," Brittany muttered. "The only person who comes off like a fool is me."

Conner leaped for her, nearly pinning her against the counter. Brittany turned her head swiftly and blinked out the side window. This was the house they'd purchased after they'd been married for a year, the house they'd raised both Valerie and Thomas in. Perhaps it was the house where he'd murder her in cold blood.

Not that he'd gotten physically violent.

Yet.

"Just tell me you understand what position you've put me in," Conner hissed. "Tell me you get it."

Brittany's voice wavered strangely. "I get it."

"Why don't I believe you?"

Brittany forced herself to lift her eyes to Conner's. With her jaw set, she listened to the mumbles of conversation outside, the squeals of babies, the swaps of funny stories about Joseph Keating, a man she would never see again.

"I'm sorry, Conner. I'm really sorry."

Brittany knew she'd been saying sorry for as long as she could remember. But it was the fastest way out of such an idiotic mess.

"There are clean shirts already ironed and hanging on the bedroom door," she told him, half-pleading with him to leave her alone. "Otherwise, you don't have to stay here any longer. You can just watch TV in the bedroom. Me and the kids will clean up here."

"Now, why would I want to leave so soon?" Conner asked, his face crumpling. "He was my father-in-law. And I want to be here. To support you. To support the kids."

Brittany held her breath until finally, Conner walked up the back staircase and headed for their bedroom. She then scrambled to pour herself a large glass of water, which she sucked down quickly. She knew she was in full-blown panic mode but hadn't any idea how to get out of it.

Brittany removed Conner's shirt from the sink and began to wash the plates and forks and sharp knives as tears rushed down her cheeks. She felt out of her mind, trying to draw up the courage to re-enter the wake and associate again with Bar Harbor residents and Joe's dearest friends.

"Need any help?" Nicole Harvey's voice rang out from the doorway.

Brittany jumped, startled, then turned the water off. She slowly turned, frightened to meet Nicole's eyes. Nicole wore a look that told Brittany she had a hunch about what had just occurred, even if she hadn't seen it up close. Had Joe told her about his opinions of Conner? Or was it something Nicole could already sense, as though Brittany was molding in the fridge?

"Naw. I'm just trying to keep up with everything," Brittany told her. "So much to do, so little time."

Nicole rolled up her sleeves and began to dry the dishes Brittany had just finished washing.

"Did Conner just go upstairs to change?" Nicole asked.

"I guess so. Not sure."

They shared the swell of silence. Nicole collected the plates in a stack and then began to dry out the knives and forks. She cleared her throat before she spoke.

"My husband, Michael... He wasn't kind to me."

Brittany's heart nearly stopped. She turned her eyes toward Nicole's as her brows furrowed. This wasn't the conversation she wanted to have at the wake of her father. This wasn't a conversation she wanted to have ever.

"I'm really sorry to hear that," Brittany told her firmly.

"I'm just saying," Nicole continued. "That one of the best things that happened to me was him leaving me for someone else. I was allowed to start over. I was allowed to be exactly myself..."

Brittany stiffened. *Who did Nicole think she was, storming in there to make Brittany believe she "knew just what she was going through?"*

19

Had Nicole even loved her husband? Did she know what it meant to love someone through the highs and lows of life?

"Thank you," Brittany told her, her voice high-pitched. "I have to go check on the snacks. Do you need anything? You let me know. Anything at all."

Brittany sprinted toward the table that held bowls of half-eaten snacks, her breath held tightly in her lungs. Two mourners stopped her to tell her what a marvelous man her father had been. She couldn't hear her voice as she told them whatever it was she'd said. Somewhere in the house, Conner waited for her. And somehow, Nicole had seen the very dynamic between them that Brittany had struggled to hide away for the previous twenty-four years of her life.

Chapter Three

Brittany's seventeen-year-old daughter, Valerie, spoke with the courage and articulation of a much more mature woman. Up to her elbows in suds in the kitchen sink, Brittany listened as Valerie spoke intently to a friend of her grandfather's who had a boatload of recommendations for the next few months of her senior year. "It's all happening right now," he informed her pointedly. "It's up to you to ride the wave. The rest of your life is about to begin. Your grandfather spoke about you with such a bright light in his eye, and he knew you were off for great things."

"I can't help but think that I'll make some kind of mistake," Valerie told him softly. "Everything's riding on the decisions I make this upcoming year."

"The beautiful thing about getting older, Valerie, is this..." the older man began. "You learn that life is all about making mistakes, and the most important part of that journey is how you pick yourself up again."

"I'm sure I won't have any trouble with that first part," Valerie offered.

"Your daughter has a real sense of humor," the older gentleman quipped toward Brittany.

Brittany turned back to catch his eye as he placed a thick wool cap over his head, sliding it gingerly over the tips of his ears. "It was a beautiful service, Brittany," he added. "We'll miss our Joe."

One after another, mourners who'd come to eat, laugh, drink, and remember had asked if there was anything left for them to help out with, anything else for them to do. When Brittany said a simple, "No," they followed one another out into the windy darkness of the autumn night, leaving just Brittany and a smattering of family and friends to help out.

"You really should take some leftovers," Brittany told Nicole pointedly as she slid an entire half of lasagna into a large Tupperware. "I'll go crazy if any of this food sticks to my thighs."

In truth: Conner made a big hissy fit when she gained anything more than a couple of pounds. *"Step right up!"* he began once when she entered a room, *"To see this winter's circus attraction! The grandest fat lady in all the land!"*

"I'll make Luke take some," Nicole said off-handily, gathering another batch of Tupperware. "Yes, he's a sous chef and shouldn't have any trouble cooking for himself. But we all know what it's like when bachelors live by themselves."

"They can't help it," Brittany teased. "Now that Thomas has moved out of the house and into his own place, I find myself worrying about what he's feeding himself. I keep thinking he's only living on mac and cheese and ramen noodles."

"Mom? What are you talking about?" Handsome Thomas stepped into the kitchen, grabbed a celery stick, and wagged it, teasing her. "Are you suggesting I'm not eating from the Food Guide Pyramid?"

To make his point, Thomas cracked the celery stick in half

with his teeth, then winced and scrunched his nose. "Gosh, what did they put in this thing? It needs more salt."

"Oh my gosh, honey." Brittany rolled her eyes as she slid a towel across a shiny wet plate. "Then it's settled. You'll take the rest of the seven-layer salad."

Against all conceivable odds, Brittany, Valerie, Thomas, Heather, and a number of other friends and family members cleaned up the rest of the house before nine. This left Brittany, Valerie, and Thomas alone in the downstairs of the old house while Conner lurked upstairs, somewhere.

"What happened to Dad?" Thomas asked, grabbing a brownie from the glass jar in the kitchen.

"He's um. Just tired. It's been a long day for all of us," Brittany tried.

Thomas's eyes flickered. "I'd say it's been a long, exhausting day for you. But that's just me."

Valerie's nostrils flared. She grabbed her phone from her purse and breezed through social media pages before collapsing on the couch to do it some more. Brittany turned her eyes toward the staircase, which glowed with the light of the upstairs bedroom. A low roar illustrated the fact that Conner played some sporting event or another.

There was no way she was going up that staircase.

"I'm going to go to the study to read for a while," Brittany told her children. "Maybe we can watch a movie later? I have a hunch that sleep won't be easy tonight."

The makeshift library-study in the Radley house was Brittany's refuge when times got tough. Conner, who'd never gone to college and had hardly lifted a book in his life (not that Brittany resented that), thought of Brittany's book collection as little more than decoration and usually scoffed when he caught her reading in there. "The game's on," he'd said more than once, as though wanting to give her a lifeline out of that fictional world.

Brittany had hand-selected an antique ochre-colored armchair for the library, mid-century, but with an extra layer of cushion that made it especially cozy on windy autumn nights. Upon the small table beside the armchair, Brittany had positioned the book her father had lent her about a month before his death— *All the Light We Cannot See* by Anthony Doerr. In the midst of the flurry of emotions and hospital visits and miscellaneous tasks that kept both herself and her family intact, Brittany hadn't had a single moment to sit down with it. Not until now, after her father's death.

After she cracked the cover, a note fluttered out from between the pages. Brittany's heart shattered at the sight of her father's handwriting. *What could it be? Some important notes? A spare thought, written down to be remembered later?* She reached for it on the carpet and lifted it, both expectant and dreading it—

And found herself holding a note from her father, scribed to Brittany.

Brittany,

It's nothing I'd tell you and Nicole up close and in person, but I have a hunch that I won't make it through the next few weeks. Such is life. I've had a good run. I've done some beautiful and not-so-beautiful things. And I've loved you and your mother madly (and I'm looking forward to seeing her up in heaven if heaven's a place I'm allowed to go).

Brittany, you were always such a wild child. Such a spitfire. Before your mother passed, I hadn't a clue what to do with you— and when she did die, I looked at you and thought, "Why me? Why does God want me to do this all alone?" In truth, it was one of my greatest pleasures, watching you come into yourself and build one of the most prosperous businesses in Bar Harbor (or maybe even the world, but what do I know? I've hardly left Bar Harbor, which is something you always loved to point out to me when you were younger).

It's also been a truly spectacular thing, watching you raise your children, my beloved grandchildren, Thomas and Valerie. I can't envision a better lineage.

Watching this wide array of beauty around you. I struggle, still, with one enormous facet of your life.

I suppose you know where I'm going with this.

When you brought Conner Radley home from your brief stint in Boston, I thought for sure it was a short-term thing. How could my beautiful, intelligent, optimistic, and goal-oriented daughter wind up with a man who clearly didn't appreciate her? I remember that first dinner when he interrupted you for the first time in front of me. Excuse me for saying this, but I wanted to kick him from the Keating House once and for all at that moment.

But I could see it in your eyes.

You already loved him. You loved him to bits. What could I do but watch and hope that things would turn out all right?

In so many ways, Brittany, they have. Things have turned out, I mean. You have two beautiful children, a gorgeous home, a profitable business.

But I hope you know that even at your age (forty-six, goodness me), you still have time to blossom and grow and change. If you don't feel that Conner gives you the space to do that, then you have to find a way to leave.

Women get up and leave their spouses every day. Women who are much less powerful than you. Women with a whole lot less to their name.

I love you, Brittany. I've loved you since that unforgettable day when you were born. And I'll love you till the day I do pass on from this earth.

How strange that I'm no longer scared of it. I look toward the future with grace, goodwill, and much love, and I'm simply thankful for all I've had.

Love,

Your Father, Joseph Keating

It was a struggle for Brittany to get through the end of the letter as her eyes welled with tears. They dotted the edge of the note, smudging the blue ink just so before she placed the note to the side. She then stared into space, her throat tightening so much that she struggled to breathe. A single sob escaped and echoed down the hallway.

And at that moment, the door creaked to bring Valerie into the library to find her.

"Mom?" Valerie had changed into pajama pants and a big t-shirt that said BAR HARBOR ATHLETICS in pink letters. She closed the door tenderly behind her and hurried to throw her arms around her mother, who continued to struggle to breathe.

"What is this?" Valerie grabbed the note and read it before Brittany could hide it from her.

To Brittany's surprise, Valerie's face hardly twitched. She seemed to re-read it, scanning her grandfather's handwriting with glittering eyes. She then sat across from her mother on the antique couch, folded her legs beneath her, and looked at her as though she was a woman of thirty rather than seventeen.

Brittany felt a strange mix of embarrassment and stoicism.

She was ready to share everything with her children.

She was ready to stop hiding behind her pride and admit her secret— that she'd married an emotionally abusive and narcissistic man.

And it was time to end it.

"Most children beg their parents to stay together," Valerie began, her voice cracking. "And maybe if I was a little bit younger, I would say something along the lines that we're a family, and that families are meant to stay together. But Mom..."

Valerie puffed out her cheeks and closed her eyes.

"Dad doesn't treat me like his special little girl anymore," she continued softly. "His cruelty has gone through you and reached me. It's usually just here and there and normally when we're alone at the house. But it's happened. And I thought to myself, '*Wow. That's what Mom has gone through all these years.*'"

Brittany's shoulders collapsed forward as she fell into another fit of tears. "I've been so stupid, Valerie. So stupid. How could you ever forgive me? For staying in this marriage? For allowing him to speak to me, and to you, like this?"

Valerie shook her head ominously. "The past is in the past, Mom. What matters is what you do now. And I'll help you with everything as we go. Okay?"

"Okay," Brittany affirmed. "I love you. I love you so much."

"I love you, too."

Chapter Four

Twenty-four years ago, after Brittany had secured the old-world place on South Main Street for her vintage and antique shop, she'd thrown herself into the business whole-heartedly— earning herself a reputation as a twenty-one-year-old entrepreneur overly-willing to put her life on the line for her dreams. Back then, during the first indications of Conner's narcissistic qualities, Brittany had crafted a plan for the redesign, staying up long nights over her draft table and assigning value to each room in the antique shop. She wanted each room to glow with a specific theme, drawing the customer deeper into its folds, into the magic of its history. She drove sometimes with Conner and other times without— across the state of Maine to inspect other antique shops, inspecting prices, floor layouts, wallpaper designs, and even the music that played in the background. She also carved a space for herself within the antique auction network of New England, becoming something of a "sight to see" as the youngest antique collector in the area.

The whispers swirled around her:

"I heard she's putting together a place in Bar Harbor."

"Should have done that myself. Bar Harbor has a killer influx of tourists during the summer months. Imagine the revenue stream..."

"I heard she got the start-up money from her father."

"Kids these days always have the upper hand. I built my business from the ground up."

"She's just a kid, and we're old fogeys. We should at least offer a helping hand. Lend our support. It's not like she's our competition all the way out east."

With seven lamps from the twenties, thirties, and forties, three couches, one from the forties, one from the fifties, and one from the sixties, several glowing antique mirrors, a thick Turkish rug, and countless vintage posters, Brittany opened her doors to Bar Harbor Antiques. She hung a banner across the front double-wide doors, played Frank Sinatra from the speakers, and served hot wine as the November winds railed against the Bar Harbor residents, casting them back indoors.

As Brittany had begun her business during the lower-trafficked autumn months rather than the vibrant summertime, her business faltered that first year. Tensions were high, both within herself and between her and Conner. He felt she'd wasted the money; he felt she should give up. But instead of doing all that, a determined Brittany rented out one-half of the downtown location to a coffee shop owner named Ygritte. This would allow her to maintain control of the space; this would give her a firmer grip on her finances.

Ygritte was a Swedish immigrant with thick luscious blonde locks, youthful skin despite her forty years, and an overall optimistic outlook on life, which she said she'd inherited from her time in the United States. "Your business has hit a difficult period of time," she told Brittany as they finalized the deal. "But that doesn't mean it's dead. You just need to nurse it back to life. Besides, I have a hunch we can help each other. I'll butter them up with coffee and snacks, and then maybe, just maybe, they'll have the energy to peruse your antiques."

That winter, Brittany moved her antiques to one side of the large building while Ygritte set up several little round, gold-lined coffee tables with delicate seats, moved in an antique counter and an espresso machine, and began concocting a menu of delightful breakfast and lunch fare (plus what seemed like a never-ending array of desserts, which Brittany avoided like the plague).

With only one-half of the rent to pay, Brittany breathed much easier and threw herself into building her brand. She only selected the antiques she felt "fit" the rest of the decor in her half of the building rather than immediately picking out the ones she knew would sell well. She didn't want to grovel to any antique pursuers. She wanted people to come and find her, specifically because she had precisely what they were looking for. Beyond that, she wanted to show people something they'd never seen before, revealing an artistry from the archives of history. She wanted her work to matter.

Over the years, Ygritte had transformed into the mother figure Brittany had ached for after the death of her own. Together, Brittany and Ygritte had worked side-by-side, yet never truly together, both operating the mechanics of their separate businesses yet also boosting one another during difficult times. Bit by bit, Brittany was able to create a denser antique collection, one that drifted closer and closer toward Ygritte's side of the building, something she always welcomed.

The October after Joseph Keating's death, while Brittany was still getting up the courage to leave her husband, Ygritte arranged for the closure of her coffee shop. It was a heartbreaking day for both Ygritte and Brittany, especially as Ygritte planned to move to Florida for the sunshine. "My old bones just can't take these Maine winters any longer," she'd explained. "And now that your business is so profitable, Brittany, there's no reason you shouldn't take up the whole building!"

Brittany had decided to take up Ygritte on this offer and had already begun to craft a plan of attack. There were auctions to attend, antiques to purchase, re-designs to begin. Throughout this time, she managed to slip just out of Conner's grasp, still avoiding the issue of the divorce she wanted. She needed courage in spades, but instead, she pummeled her energy into Bar Harbor Antiques.

Valerie had agreed to take over the espresso counter on Saturdays and Sundays as a way to pick up extra cash during her senior year. This meant that the coffee shop portion of the building would remain in place, but the antiques would flourish all around the smaller coffee-shop area, making it seem straight from a history textbook of a forgotten time.

"Gosh, we'll miss you." Brittany draped her arms around Ygritte's tiny frame as she closed shop for the final time.

Beside Brittany, Valerie clung to a huge bouquet of flowers, which she passed to Ygritte along with a tearful, "I hope you'll come to visit us?"

Ygritte pressed a kiss on Valerie's forehead. Brittany's heart surged with memories. Ygritte had been here for every enormous milestone— her marriage to Conner, the birth of Thomas and then Valerie, her first big antique sales. *What would she do without her?*

"It feels like the end of an era," Brittany breathed as she pressed the door open for Ygritte, who stepped into the gloom of a grey October afternoon.

"It's up to you to decide what the next era holds," Ygritte told her, raising an eyebrow mysteriously. "And I know you have it in you, Brittany. You've always been a fighter."

* * *

After Ygritte left for good, Valerie and Brittany returned to the large space and analyzed the enormity of the echoing emptiness. "We need to fill all of this space," Brittany said, looking at every inch of the room. "Otherwise, people will come in here and wonder who robbed us."

Valerie chuckled good-naturedly. She walked behind the counter, hunting for the brownies Ygritte had left behind. "You said there was an auction this weekend?"

Brittany's throat tightened. She hadn't been to an auction since early summer, before Joseph Keating's health had declined significantly. Back then, Conner had been around to help, his tongue sharp with soft insults but his arms ready to carry whatever needed to be hauled. She hadn't yet asked for a divorce, but she didn't feel up to spending a weekend away with him, either.

"I don't know if I'm up for it," Brittany admitted.

Valerie shook her head, seeming surer of herself than Brittany ever had in her life. "No way. We're going. I'll drive you there if I have to, and we'll pay people to carry our things." She added the last part with a shrug, as though she could read her mother's mind. "They always have helpers waiting in the wings at those things."

Brittany knew her daughter was right.

That Friday afternoon, Brittany picked up her daughter from Bar Harbor High School and sped west toward Lewiston, the second-largest city in Maine. Valerie waited for her mother out on the cracked sidewalk with her hands wrapped tightly around the straps of her backpack. The sharp wind caught her dark brown locks and whipped them around her cheeks. She raised an arm to greet her mother, then slid into the front of Brittany's SUV, dropping the backpack into the back with a huff.

How different it was, picking Valerie up as a seventeen-year-old. It seemed that only a few seconds before, she'd been too frightened to cross the road without holding Brittany's hand.

"There she is. My senior! All grown up!"

"You're funny, Mom. I'm so tired of school!"

Brittany dropped her foot on the pedal and eased out of the after-school traffic, which was always a chaotic mess and a blare of horns. She remembered herself as a senior, feeling that graduation day couldn't come fast enough. She couldn't say that she longed for those days— but she did want to tell Valerie not to wish away her life. It all went too quickly, she thought.

"I heard from Ygritte," Brittany announced as soon as they merged onto the highway. "She's all moved into her bungalow in Naples. Just a ten-minute walk to the beach. She says we should visit her when we find the time."

Valerie's eyes flashed excitedly. "Florida? I've hardly ever left Maine."

Brittany's heart bruised at the words. She could practically hear herself saying them, twenty-five years ago. Had she turned into her father? A Bar Harbor "born and bread" who hadn't bothered to see the world?

"I've thought about applying to a few schools outside of New England," Valerie announced.

"Oh!" Brittany's heart jumped into her throat. Valerie hadn't mentioned anything like this until now. There had been talk of the University of Maine, the University of Vermont. Nothing too far, and nothing outside of the realm of their own lives. But she wasn't in any position to build walls around her daughter's life. "What um... What sorts of places?"

Valerie listed out a few options, including New York University and the University of Chicago, both of which seemed on the other end of the earth.

"You know, my cousin, Heather's daughters, live in New York City," Brittany explained.

"Yeah, of course. Kristine and Bella. But isn't 'cousin Heather' not your cousin at all?" Valerie quipped.

"Yes, well. She's still my cousin for all intents and purposes, and she's still a part of the family," Brittany returned.

Only recently, they learned that Uncle Adam wasn't Heather's father, that Casey and Nicole weren't Heather's sisters at all. Heather had come to Bar Harbor to discover more about her family— and in turn, she'd discovered a world of pain and sorrow.

Even still, it was probably better to know the truth. Wasn't it?

* * *

The following morning before the auction, Brittany and Valerie awoke around five-thirty, showered, dressed in their Sunday best, and drove out to the warehouse on the outer edge of Lewiston, where the auction was being held prior to an after-noon party for antique collectors and antique shop owners across the state. Brittany had set out a plan for exactly what she'd planned to bid on but also allowed herself to be surprised by the collection, which featured a number of tables, chairs, couches, lamps, and wardrobes from the fifties and seventies— two of her favorite eras of design.

Brittany was a confident bidder. It was a skill she'd had to take on over the previous decades as she'd built up her business, one that demanded respect from other antique sellers and buyers alike. Over the course of the morning, she bid on item after item, securing three of the six items she'd come to Lewiston for and one surprise object, a wardrobe with ornate floral carvings.

"Nice work, Mom," Valerie whispered under her breath as they stood for a mid-morning break. "That guy behind you was fuming that you got the wardrobe. You pushed him just a little too high."

Brittany, who was high off the bidding race as though she'd just run a marathon, rubbed her palms together excitedly. She then muttered, "I had this feeling he was about to break. A sixth sense, if you will."

Valerie laughed good-naturedly and pointed toward the coffee table in the corner. "You want anything to eat? A muffin, maybe?"

"I can't eat. It could throw me off," Brittany replied. "Sugar makes me soft."

"Okay. You're sounding like a psycho now," Valerie teased. "I'm going to grab two muffins and two coffees. You can have yours now or later. Your choice."

Brittany walked toward the wardrobe she'd just purchased, circling it and marveling at all the delicate detail. She thought she could get at least two thousand for it, as it was quite large and spectacular, nothing like anything she'd seen before. Two thousand, five-hundred, maybe. Sometimes it was difficult to gauge what people would spend for truly iconic pieces. *Was three thousand too much?*

Brittany stepped out from her circular pattern and, distracted, ran headlong into a passing security guard. She bucked back, surprised, and said, "Oh gosh. I'm so sorry."

It was almost exactly what had happened with Conner— running into him, so distracted. Had this been Conner, he'd have already hurled a number of insults directly into her ear.

But as their eyes met, the security guard delivered the most generous and sterling smile she'd ever seen. A feeling of innocence and beauty stirred within her, a feeling she hadn't felt in many, many years.

"Don't you worry about it," he told her.

Brittany's smile widened. "I really didn't mean..."

"Don't," the security guard cut her off. "It was my fault for passing by so quickly."

Brittany arched her eyebrow in surprise. Did he want to take the blame himself? It felt outside the bounds of reason. A moment of silence passed between them.

"You're Brittany Radley, aren't you?" The security guard brushed a dark strand of hair behind his ear nervously.

"Umm...yes. Has the gossip mill around here talked about me?"

"No, not at all. I'm a cop in Bar Harbor," he continued. "My sister's involved with the antique circuit and often recruits me to work as a security guard at these things. I've passed your store and had a coffee or two in the coffee shop that's attached to it."

"Huh, well, that's good to know." Brittany furrowed her brow. "It's a rare thing that I meet a Bar Harbor resident I don't know."

"I'm a relative newcomer," he informed her. "I fell in love with the area, though. I think I've scoured just about every trail in Acadia National Park."

Valerie appeared beside Brittany with two carrot muffins and two steaming coffees, which she carried with difficulty. "Hot! Hot!" she cried out as Brittany collected hers.

"Listen," the security guard continued. "Let me know if you need any help loading any of your antiques later on. I know they can be real annoyances. But after all this work on the antique circuit for my sister, at least I know what kind of trouble I'm getting myself into..."

Brittany's eyes widened with surprise. *Who was this man? Why did he care so much? Was this just how decent people acted?*

"I'll let you know, thanks," she said. "What was your name?"

"Brad," the cop told her, sticking out a large, smooth, masculine hand. "Brad Wethers."

"Well, hello, Brad Wethers. It's very nice to meet you," Brittany told him, her voice catching in her throat. "I'm happy I ran into you earlier and even happier I didn't have a coffee in my hand yet."

"You and me both," Brad returned with a laugh. "Hot coffee is a real danger to us all."

"And that's coming from a cop." Brittany teased.

The auctioneer returned to the front pulpit and announced the bidding would commence once more. Brittany sipped her coffee and nodded goodbye as Brad Wethers returned to his stance at the back end of the large spacious warehouse. Valerie jabbed her mother in the side, nearly making the coffee fling from her hand.

"What. Was. That?" Valerie demanded as they returned to their seats.

"Just some neighborly kindness," Brittany replied with a shrug. "He's a cop in Bar Harbor, and said he'd been to Ygritte's shop."

"Yeah?" Valerie looked doubtful as she turned to watch him. "I didn't know they made cops that handsome in Bar Harbor..."

"Valerie!" Brittany chided as her heart made another flip in her chest. "We're going to get kicked out of the auction if we don't quiet down."

But inwardly, Brittany's heart swelled with what seemed like hope. As her antique selection widened, as she took over the other half of the shop, and as she forced herself into the world alone, she found herself filling with confidence she'd forgotten since her youth.

Her marriage was truly over. She was done.

And she was more than ready for the rest of her life to begin.

Chapter Five

It was a funny coincidence that the divorce lawyer Brittany contacted early that November was none other than Mary, the woman she'd run off to Boston with over twenty years before. Immediately after their stint in Boston, Mary had struck out for law school, where she'd met her husband, Josh, and had two babies, even in the midst of all-night study sessions and semester finals. Mary and Josh had returned to Bar Harbor only five years before. Despite that, their friendship had stalled. Brittany had felt trapped in her marriage to Conner and unwilling to show the truth of her sorrows, especially not to Mary, who'd been around since the very beginning.

When Brittany entered Mary's law office, her chin lifted and her mind made-up, Mary opened her arms to her once-dearest friend and said, "Whatever it is, we'll fix it. But you have to tell me the truth for once."

Mary listened intently as Brittany outlined the entire story, beginning from the autumn when Conner had arrived in Bar Harbor to their very short engagement, the first house they purchased, the birth of their babies, and the mental and emotional abuse that had only escalated over the years.

"It got so bad that I sometimes felt I couldn't get up in the morning," Brittany told Mary sheepishly. "And you know me. That's the furthest thing from my personality."

"You were always one of the biggest go-getters I knew," Mary affirmed, removing her glasses from the bridge of her nose and twirling them. "Let me ask you this, Brittany... Do you trust him not to fly off the handle when you tell him you want a divorce?"

Brittany shook her head slowly. "I have no idea what he will do."

Mary scribed something to herself on a notepad then clicked through several pages on her computer. "I would recommend having a potential restraining order in place," Mary began. "You can tell him about it coolly and say that you'd prefer not to use it, but it's an option for you."

Brittany stuttered with disbelief. "I don't know if that's necessary..."

Mary flashed Brittany a dark look. "Based on everything you've just told me, Conner doesn't care about your mental or emotional health. You also said that he's frightened you physically a number of times. This is not a man that you want anywhere near you. After you tell him to leave your home, I suggest that you speak only through me, your lawyer, and never directly to him. These narcissists can be incredibly manipulative. If you give them an inch, they take the whole yard."

Brittany knew Mary was right. She let her shoulders fall forward as she sat, genuinely shocked that she'd finally taken this step forward. Valerie would be so proud of her.

But mostly, dammit, Brittany was proud of herself.

"How do you plan to tell him?" Mary asked pointedly.

"I..."

"Because I would suggest having someone there with you,"

Mary continued. "Someone who has your back. Probably someone male."

Brittany arranged for Luke, the sous chef from the Keating Inn and Acadia Eatery, to arrive at her home the following afternoon, a little bit before Conner was slated to return from his workday. She hadn't told him specifically what she was up to— only that she needed his help for something her father had wanted her to do long ago. Luke wasn't the sort to poke and prod at something he sensed you didn't want to talk about. That was the beauty of Luke.

At three-fifteen, Valerie arrived home from school. There was the sound of the screeching door, and then a backpack plopped on the couch. Valerie then made her way into the kitchen to grab a snack, where she found Brittany with her hands stretched out wide across the counter, her legs quivering beneath her.

"Mom!"

Brittany snapped her head upright to meet Valerie's eyes. "Hi, honey." Her voice seemed several miles away.

"You good?" Valerie hustled to pour her mother a glass of water, which she pressed into her hand. "What's up? I'm surprised you're not at the store."

Brittany closed her eyes as she sucked down one-half of the glass of water. When she returned the glass to the counter, she breathed, "I'm going to tell your father that I want a divorce today."

Valerie stiffened and then took a step back. Her face played out the her wild emotions— regret, fear, sorrow, and a slight hint of gratefulness.

"Okay," Valerie breathed, giving Brittany a subtle nod. "Okay."

"Luke's supposed to come to be a backup," Brittany explained. "He should get here in a few minutes, before your father..."

But just then, the front door slammed open and two male voices beamed out, speaking confidently, brightly about a recent football game. Brittany knew these voices like the back of her hand. It was Thomas and his father, Conner. Perhaps they'd decided to leave work early. Thomas, who hadn't stopped in to say hello to his mother in over a week, had decided today was the day.

Great.

But there was no going back now. Brittany had come this far. She'd slated this day as the first of the rest of her life.

Valerie gave her a bug-eyed look. Brittany lifted her chin, resolute, and called out, "Hello? Do I hear Thomas?"

Her handsome son stepped through the kitchen doorway with his muscular arms outstretched. He'd recently showered after his stint on the lobster boat. His hair was slightly damp and his skin hinted the slightest bit of salt. Brittany hugged him a little too hard, as this was the last hug she would share with her son when the Radley Family was still the Radley Family.

They could never go back.

"Hi, honey." Conner stepped in after Thomas, then grabbed a beer from the fridge and cracked it open, wearing a crooked smile. "Thomas and I met with some new clients today. The boy has real sales talent, and I told him he gets it from his mama." Conner winked at her, that delirious wink that used to make her weak in the knees, but now made her skin crawl.

This was the thing about narcissists, Mary had told her. *'You give them an inch, they take a yard.'*

"What's up with you?" Conner finally asked. "You're awful quiet."

Thomas grabbed a beer from the fridge, following after his father, then smacked Valerie playfully on the shoulder. Brittany adored the friendship her children had with one another. *Would the divorce destroy that?*

41

"Brittany. I asked you a question," Conner told her firmly.

"Do you mind if we talk?" Brittany asked, her voice catching. "Just for a minute."

"We're all here," Conner replied. "There's nothing you can say to me that you can't say to the kids."

Brittany wanted to point out how ridiculous that was— that their children were seventeen and nineteen and not totally privy to the privacy of their lives. That said, maybe it was better if she did this in front of them. Maybe he wouldn't fly off the handle so quickly... Just maybe.

"Okay." Brittany crossed and took a step back. "Okay then. I'd like to tell you that I met with a divorce lawyer yesterday. And I'd like to begin the separation proceedings and, ultimately, a divorce."

In all her years of knowing the manipulative and cruel Conner Radley, Brittany Keating had never seen him quite like this.

All the color in his face immediately drained, leaving it stark white. His hands clenched tightly over his beer, making the can crackle. There was a wicked flash in the back of his eyes, proof that something had broken within him— something that couldn't be repaired.

Almost immediately, a voice in the back of Brittany's head demanded of her: *What have you done?*

"Is this how you're going to do this, huh?" Conner began, his nostrils flared. "You're going to destroy our family? Everything we've built? The minute you have more success with your business, you're going to say you've had just about enough of me? You're ready to get rid of this?"

Suddenly, Conner flailed his free hand skyward and smashed it on the counter. Valerie nearly leaped out of her skin. Brittany, accustomed to Conner's flair-ups, hardly flinched.

"Dad..." Thomas began, trying to reason with him. Thomas

adored his father, at least when they were getting along, but Brittany had seen their relationship go south more than once.

"I've already begun the process of getting a restraining order," Brittany added coolly. "It's been suggested to me that we communicate only through our lawyers from now on."

"A restraining order? Jesus Christ, Brittany." A number of other expletives flew from his mouth as he reached for the toaster, yanked it from the wall, and flung it across the room with a tremendous crash.

The toaster had narrowly missed hitting Thomas in the side of the head.

"What the hell!" Thomas cried. He reached out to grab Valerie, drawing her into the room directly beside the kitchen.

"Where the hell am I supposed to go, Brittany?" Conner howled. "This is my home! We bought it together!"

"We can work out the details of that with the lawyer," Brittany countered simply. She felt like she was outside of her body, as though she was a puppet and someone far away played with the strings. "I imagine it won't be difficult to work out some sort of arrangement. People get divorced all the time."

"People get divorced all the time." Conner mimicked her angrily, then grabbed the coffee pot and flailed it across the kitchen. The glass shattered and flung across the ground.

In the next room, Valerie screamed. Brittany hustled for her, suddenly frightened. She wasn't entirely sure what to do with a toddler-like husband in the next room, eager to hurl whatever he found at them. He could destroy everything in the kitchen— and then what? Move on to the dining room? The living room? Remove the television from the wall and smash it against the ground?

But unbeknownst to Brittany, Thomas had been in the hallway, already on the phone with the police for the previous thirty seconds. He indicated this with a pointed finger toward his cell. Over the next two minutes of Conner Radley's breakdown, Brittany waited with bated breath, listening for the sound of the sirens. When they came, Thomas rushed for the door and opened it, gesturing for them to enter as quickly as possible.

The cops who'd arrived were friendly already with Conner Radley. They'd drank with him at the local bar, nodded to him at the community fairs, caught up with him at soccer games back in the day, and generally thought of him as just another "family man" in Bar Harbor. Brittany would learn later that most people just assumed what they wanted to assume. Conner was handsome, loyal, friendly, and strong. Not the portrait of an abuser.

"Conner! We need you to calm down," one of the cops said as he entered the kitchen, his swagger powerful and demanding attention.

"Who said you could enter my house?" Conner demanded. "Who let you in?"

"We were notified of a domestic dispute," the cop told him.

Brittany turned to face Valerie and drew her arms around her daughter, who quivered against her. It had all gone so terribly wrong. But at least, now, it was over. At least now, they could move forward.

Just then, another figure entered the Radley House. Luke hustled toward the dining room, his eyes wide. "What happened?" he demanded. "I'm so sorry. I didn't know I was late."

"He got home early," Brittany replied simply, as Conner's rage escalated in the next room. "It couldn't be helped."

Together, Brittany, Thomas, Luke, and Valerie watched as the cops escorted Conner out of the house. The first cop who'd arrived sat down with them to get their statements. When he learned that Brittany was already in the process of getting a restraining order, he breathed a sigh of relief.

"I have a hunch that Conner Radley won't be welcomed in

Bar Harbor after today," he said simply. "We don't want those kinds of folks around here."

After the cop car sped back toward the station with Conner Radley in back, the remaining family members swept up the debris from Conner's breakdown, ordered a pizza, and slowly found a way to speak through the horrific pain of that fateful afternoon. Brittany knew it would take time to wade through this and come out the other side. But she felt sure of herself, of her children, and of their combined strength. They had to make it work, and they would. That was that.

Chapter Six

Present Day

It was the first day of April, a Friday. Brittany Keating gripped the handles of a stationary bike as the downtown YMCA instructor, the one with the amazing behind, demanded the class to keep striving and keep pedaling. "You've got to dig down deep! Push yourself harder than you've pushed yourself before! Don't you want this? Prove it to me!" Brittany's thighs screamed; sweat poured down her back and caked against her tank top. But when the clock struck six-thirty a.m. and the class was over, she erupted from the bike seat with a glistening, sweaty smile on her face. She'd done it.

"Nice work, Britt." This was the instructor, who'd singlehandedly sculpted Brittany from a size eight to a size five since Brittany's decision to join spin class in January.

"Thanks. Now I'll try not to destroy all that hard work this weekend. My family's having a little get-together tonight... and my cousins really know how to pour the wine. On top of that,

Valerie and I are headed to Upstate New York for an auction, and I'm sure we won't be eating salads the whole time."

The instructor chuckled good-naturedly and reminded Brittany, "We have to live between the work-outs. Otherwise, what's all this working out for?"

Twenty minutes later, Brittany walked out into the chill of the early morning, drove back to the house where she and Valerie now lived together alone, and found her daughter in the midst of making them both a healthy, low-carb breakfast of eggs and avocados and vibrant, sliced tomatoes. Coffee bubbled and spat into the pot, newly purchased after Conner's destruction the previous November. All of that seemed like somebody else's life, now.

"How was spin class?" Valerie asked brightly.

"Invigorating, like always." Brittany took a large sip from her water bottle. "You should really come with me sometime."

"Get up at five-fifteen? I don't think so," Valerie joked.

Brittany and Valerie sat at the kitchen table, sipping coffee and eating their breakfast, talking about the weekend ahead, including the auction that began Saturday afternoon. After school, Valerie had a short meeting regarding various graduation activities, including the Senior Picnic, Senior Pool Party, and the Senior Prom. The following week was Valerie's spring break, which meant that soon, she'd be in the home stretch of her schooling. Unlike most of her classmates, she still hadn't decided on a university.

"It's hard to believe it's all about to happen." Brittany breathed. "When your brother graduated two years ago, he wasn't interested in all the celebration stuff. I barely got him to pick up his cap and gown."

"I wouldn't do that to you," Valerie assured her mother. "I know you want to celebrate just as much as me. Probably more."

Brittany had recently purchased a second-hand vehicle for

Valerie. A Chevy Cavalier made six years before. Brittany watched from the front window as Valerie slid into the front seat, started the engine, and eased out from the driveway. Each time she watched her leave, Brittany said a little internal prayer for Valerie's safety.

Because really, if Brittany was honest with herself, she was waiting for something to go wrong. Since Conner had been led out of their home the previous November, she hadn't caught a single glimpse of him. He'd arranged to have his things packed up and taken to wherever it was he chose to stay. On top of that, he'd communicated with a divorce lawyer who'd maintained contact with Brittany's divorce lawyer, just as Brittany had asked. According to Thomas, Conner had quit his job and hadn't contacted him whatsoever, which had made things rather awkward for Thomas, who still worked there. Still, Thomas was grateful for the job and said that bit-by-bit, it was as though his father had never worked there at all.

Conner had leaped out of their lives without question and seemed uninterested in making any contact, even with his children.

Since Ygritte's decision to move to Florida, Brittany had slowly built up the building on South Main, filling bits of the gaps that Ygritte had left behind. She'd also maintained the coffee bar, including various sandwiches, snacks, and desserts. Despite her urgent search for more antiques from the forties, fifties, sixties, and seventies, Brittany hadn't yet capitalized on the other half of the building and regretted it, as the space still felt cavernous and unused. When she admitted this to one of her cousins or her daughter, they usually scoffed at her and said something like, "*Come on. You've been through a lot this past winter. Take it easy on yourself— and wait till spring to make things happen.*"

Brittany entered Bar Harbor Antiques that morning at nine to find that, already, Gabe, the barista who worked weekdays, was already set-up and ready-to-go, an espresso for her already in hand.

"Gabe. You're always so early!" Brittany said as she accepted the drink.

Gabe, a twenty-four-year-old painter who'd moved to Bar Harbor for the scenery, blushed and said, "You know I'm a terrible sleeper. I got up this morning around four to work on a painting and then came in around eight to set up. I also hung up a few more of my paintings." He gestured toward the wall, where his collection of angry seas and stoic lighthouses and glowing rocks hung. Brittany was grateful for the paintings, as she felt they added a worthy ambiance to the space.

"I love them, Gabe," she breathed. "You're so talented."

"Tell that to the MFA program that just declined my application..." Gabe returned with a sigh.

"They're idiots," she shot. "Plain and simple."

"At least I have this job," Gabe said. "I'd be lost without it."

"I wanted to ask you, Gabe." Brittany began. "Would you mind being at the warehouse Sunday evening? Valerie and I will be purchasing a bunch of antiques Saturday, and I'm paying a mover to have them delivered so that we can stretch out our girls' trip. Of course, I'll pay you double your hourly wage since it's so sudden and on the weekend to boot."

Gabe blushed and stuttered in that nervous way of his, saying, "Gosh, of course. I'll be on-call. Just let me know when to be at the warehouse."

The warehouse was what they called the back building attached to this one, with a back exit that led into the alleyway. It was a high-ceilinged building, which Brittany had hardly used over the years, as she hadn't had enough inventory to spill into the back. Now with the front building all her own and much more money than she'd ever had before, she needed to fill that space immediately.

With this expansion, she knew she also needed to hire more

employees and boost her advertising revenue. How she'd operated before, when Conner had held her back, wasn't how she
planned to operate now. She wanted people to drive from states
over to visit her store. She wanted to be on the "Best of Bar
Harbor" lists. She wanted to be one of those "successful
women" she read about in magazines— women like her cousins,
the Harvey Sisters.

Brittany headed in back to answer emails, check inventory,
and plan out the weekend's trip to upstate New York. She also
sent another email to her insurance provider to ask about
expanding her insurance coverage. Her insurance coverage as
of now was almost good enough given some sort of disaster— a
fire or a flood or something like that. But once she got the new
inventory in, her insurance coverage was akin to wearing a rain-
coat in a hurricane. It wasn't even close to being good enough.

A few minutes later, her insurance provider messaged back
to say that the insurance would be cleared in two weeks' time.
Brittany groaned inwardly but then shifted her sights toward
optimism. So, she hadn't gotten the insurance changed in time.
In her twenty-five years of business ownership, hardly anything
had gone wrong. She tried to think of the worst things and
came up with a few— Ygritte burning herself on a drop baking
sheet, Brittany breaking her toe on an old wardrobe, a younger
Valerie falling off the top of a dresser (which she'd been told not
to play on). That was basically it.

Back in the main part of the shop, Brittany assisted an older
couple on their quest to redecorate the sitting room in the new
home they'd purchased on the shoreline. They spoke of their
recent retirement and their lifelong dream to live in Bar
Harbor.

"I love these kinds of stories," Brittany told them, wearing a
brilliant smile. "All your lives, you've allowed yourselves to
dream. And now, you've made that dream a reality."

Ultimately, Brittany helped them pick out a gorgeous dark

green couch from the sixties, an antique lamp, and a painting made by Gabe himself. The bill rang up to eight hundred and seventeen dollars, including tax. This was more than triple the cost of keeping the entire place open that day. Brittany's heart swelled with gladness.

* * *

Several hours later, Brittany and Valerie met outside the Keating House after their parallel "long days," both grateful to be finished and ready for the weekend ahead. Even from the front porch of the Keating House, they listened to the wild hubbub within, the chaotic conversation from the Harvey Sisters, Luke, Luke's new-found sister, Angie, along with her pregnant daughter, Hannah, who was around five months along.

"Are you ready for this?" Brittany asked Valerie.

"Ready as I'll ever be."

Together, they burst through the front door to discover the gorgeous scene: champagne and wine bottles open, platters lined with sausages and stinky slabs of cheese, beautiful Spanish olives in bowls, and a beautiful dish of roasted stuffed peppers in the oven. The party was meant to celebrate breaking ground on the newly-planned Keating House, which was the house where Casey and her husband, Grant, planned to live, located closer to the forest line but still on the Keating property.

Heather clapped with excitement, rushing toward them to kiss their cheeks.

"I'm so glad you made it!" she cried excitedly, guiding them deeper into the kitchen.

"I thought you said you were off for an auction this week-end?" Nicole asked happily.

"We don't leave till tomorrow," Valerie explained.

"And it's not like we wanted to miss this celebration," Brittany said as Luke passed her a glass of wine. She lifted it toward Casey and said, "Congratulations on breaking ground. I can't believe this property has such life to it these days, especially after growing up here with only my daddy. This space felt so gloomy. So lonely."

"We talk about that sometimes," Nicole admitted, her voice only a murmur. "And worry that we're encroaching on your space..."

"Nonsense," Brittany told her, truly meaning it. "I love that the three of you came back to Bar Harbor, learned more about Adam, and took on responsibilities at the Keating Inn. I said it over and over, but I never wanted anything to do with it."

"It's changed quite a bit over the years," Nicole pointed out. "Especially now that we have jazz nights with Angie."

Angie blushed as she stroked a carrot through a big bowl of hummus. "Lots of musical talent around here. It hasn't been so difficult, finding people to play with. And the tips in Bar Harbor are nothing to scoff at."

Angie, too, was in the midst of a divorce from a husband who remained out west in Chicago. She'd discovered he was having an affair with another member of the jazz band they'd started years before. Brittany, Angie, and Nicole sometimes called themselves the "*divorcée club*," speaking about the devastation about moving on from someone you'd once thought was your everything. By contrast, Casey had worked things out with her husband, and Heather's husband had passed on. Strange what life did to you.

Brittany selected a small slab of spicy Camembert and slid it across a grain cracker as Casey told a story from the breaking ground event earlier that morning. Grant placed his arm easily around her as she spoke, and she occasionally lifted her eyes toward his, catching his gaze. Theirs was true love, a textured love, a love worth fighting for.

That moment, there was a knock at the door. Nicole sprung for it as Heather guffawed. "Who did you invite, Nicole?" But they soon had their answer. Evan Snow appeared with a bottle of wine in-hand and a strange smile across his lips. Brittany shivered at the sight of him. Nicole, who continued to pretend that the two of them were "only friends," said that Evan just wanted to "stop by to say congratulations on the breaking of ground."

Heather and Casey had spoken to Brittany about Nicole's fledgling "non-relationship" with Evan Snow several times. Nicole was very sparse with her words about her feelings for him. And it was clear, too, that Evan Snow had been instrumental in providing the funds that allowed the Keating Inn and Acadia Eatery to continue to remain open, even after his brother, Elijah, had attempted to seize the property.

Even still, Brittany didn't trust Evan Snow.

There was the fact that if you grew up a Bar Harbor "born and bred," you had a strange relationship with the Snow family. They took all they could and refused to give back; they were manipulative and cruel and had little thought for the poorer people in town.

But beyond that, both Elijah and Evan Snow had been friendly with her husband, Conner.

She wasn't entirely sure how that friendship had begun. Conner had been an outsider, working as a lobster fisherman. Probably, he'd sold lobster to one of the restaurants that the Snow Brothers owned, had a beer with them, and found common ground of manipulation and greed. He'd been so dashing, so whip-smart. It was a rare thing not to fall head-over-heels.

But now that Conner was gone and Nicole was apparently so chummy with Evan Snow, Brittany wasn't sure where she stood with Evan. She hadn't seen anything of Elijah, either. Heather suggested that Evan and Elijah were no longer speaking, but Brittany wasn't so sure. Snow blood ran deep. She warned the Harvey Sisters to be hesitant.

"Let's eat, shall we?" Nicole announced excitedly, her beautiful eyes flickering up toward Evan Snows.

"It looks like you've outdone yourself yet again, chef," Luke teased as they sat around the beautiful antique table.

It was the very same table where Brittany's father had met Conner all those years ago.

But times had changed.

"To the brand-new Keating House," Heather announced, lifting her glass of wine toward Casey and then toward the window that faced the back of the property. "I'm so excited about the beautiful life we're building here. I'm so excited about the future, with all of you by my side."

Chapter Seven

The drive from Bar Harbor, Maine, to the town of Lake George, New York, was slated to take approximately seven hours and thirty-two minutes. For this journey, Brittany and Valerie loaded up on both salty and sugary snacks, diet cokes, downloaded podcasts and albums, and plenty of gossip, which they'd saved for this special occasion. Although the mother-daughter duo had become thicker than thieves over the previous months since Conner's departure, they'd promised to save special stories for this very trip to keep it interesting.

"It doesn't matter when we break into the Cheez-Its, does it?" Valerie tugged open the plastic bag to dig into the salty, cheesy snack, which she crunched evenly, joy permeating her face.

"It's nine a.m.!" Brittany cried.

"So what?" Valerie demanded.

"So... It's Cheez-It-Time, is what," Brittany quipped as she splayed out her palm. "Cheez-It me, please. And tell me more about this prom drama."

Valerie puffed out her cheeks as she explained the over-whelming drama surrounding none other than Maddy Snow, Evan Snow's youngest daughter, and her recent spontaneous and very public breakup. The boy she'd dumped had assisted her in stealing Luke's sailboat the previous October, which, in Brittany's mind, had labeled Maddy as "just another Snow."

"She called him a cheating b-word," Valerie explained. "But this other guy hovered in front of her, protecting her. I think the real story is that Maddy cheated on him and then invented a story that he cheated on her first."

"That's classic," Brittany returned. "Blame the victim."

"Yeah, well. It was a whole lot of drama before first period," Valerie affirmed. "And Maddy stormed off school property after that. I guess the principal had to call Evan Snow in to talk about what had happened. I wonder if Nicole knows about it?"

"I'm not really sure what Nicole's relationship with Evan Snow is, to be honest with you," Brittany admitted, heaving a sigh. "You're eighteen now. I would tell you if I knew more. All I know is she should really be careful. I don't trust those Snow brothers."

"Especially because they were friends with Dad, right?"

Brittany's nostrils flared. It was a rare thing that she and Valerie brought up Conner. In fact, they basically pretended that he was non-existent, as though Valerie and Thomas had been the result of immaculate conception.

"I guess so," Brittany replied somberly, rolling her shoulders back.

"We don't have to talk about him," Valerie added hurriedly.

"No. It's probably better that we do. He's not the Boogey Man. He's just... a terribly lost soul," Brittany tried. "And I hope he figures everything out. Wherever he is."

Silence fell as Valerie reached forward to search around for a good radio station. She flickered around, finding mostly static until she landed on a song called "Easy on Me" by Adele. A thing Brittany adored about having a teenager, especially this deep into her forties, was that she felt constantly in tune with what was happening in the real world. If she'd been alone in the SUV, she might have played something from her teenage years, something she and Mary might have jammed out to on that drive to Boston, before everything changed.

"And what about you?" Brittany said after Adele's soulful voice faded out.

"What about me?"

"What about your prom date?"

"I don't have a prom date," Valerie returned simply.

Brittany arched an eyebrow and shifted her face ever-so-slightly toward her daughter, maintaining one eye on the road. How could she tell her daughter how beautiful she was without sounding like beauty was the only thing that mattered? How could she tell her how worthy of romance and love she was without sounding silly?

"Do you have anyone you'd like to ask?" Brittany finally asked.

"Nope." Valerie crossed her arms over her chest, an indication that the conversation was over.

Brittany dropped her teeth into her bottom lip as fear swelled in her stomach. Had her horrible relationship with Conner given Valerie some idea that love wasn't worth it? Thomas had dated on and off, but boys were different. They didn't always read into things the way girls did.

"I'd just like to go with my girlfriends," Valerie told Brittany firmly, as though she could feel the thoughts swimming in Brittany's head. "It's more fun that way. Also, have you ever tried talking to a teenage boy? They don't have many interesting things to say. And that's putting it lightly."

Brittany chose to laugh at her daughter's joke rather than dispute it. She then pointed toward a package of chips located near Valerie's feet and said, "Why don't you crack those open? I want a Cheez-It, chip combo."

"Wow. The ultimate experiment," Valerie teased. "You're brave."

* * *

Brittany and Valerie arrived at the Lake George auctioneer warehouse at just past three-thirty in the afternoon. It was a gorgeous day, with a full arc of blue sky above, bustling tree limbs with the first shock of green buds, and cow farms in every direction, painting a beautiful portrait of old-world country life.

As Brittany entered the warehouse, they greeted everyone with warm smiles. Several of them whispered what seemed to be gossip into one another's ears. Brittany liked to think they regretted that Brittany had made the drive over, as she had a killer sense of design and enough money to throw around these days to make everyone else nervous. This wasn't a game to her, per se, but she liked to win. With Conner out of the picture, Brittany saw no reason why she couldn't win as much as she pleased, as long as she set her sights on it.

Valerie and Brittany sat off to the left of the arranged seats and waited as the auctioneer assembled himself at the front of the warehouse. Two muscular men wheeled out the first item, an eighteenth-century wardrobe on which someone had painted a horrific picture of a rooster. Brittany almost laughed at the ridiculous nature of it. Who would actually buy that?

To her surprise, a number of people wanted it.

In fact, the bidding paraded all the way up to four thousand one hundred dollars. Brittany breathed into Valerie's ear, saying, "Who would ever buy that?"

To this, Valerie answered, "You always said you didn't care

about what anyone wanted to buy in your store. You only cared what fit your aesthetic."

"Yes, but... Who in their right mind has a rooster aesthetic?"

"Shhh," someone shushed her from far off to the right as another antique piece was wheeled to the center and the bidding began once more.

Valerie nudged her mother playfully, wagging her eyebrows. Brittany's heart lifted. She felt suddenly like a teenager in a high school class, goofing off. What fun to be forty-six yet feeling like the world was there, right at her fingertips.

Brittany had done her research and, true to her vision, bid to her heart's content.

First, there was the Italian three-seat sofa, which had been designed in the style of Gio Ponti. It had been made in the year 1953 and ultimately sold to her for six-hundred and fifty dollars. As she'd expected to sell it for a little more than one thousand, she thought this was a fair price.

After that came a much heftier bid. There it was— a semi-circular corner sofa, velvet, colored a light salmon. Brittany shivered as she forced her baton up to bid on it. Very soon, she found herself in a heavy bidding war with a collector based in Vermont. Finally, she beat him out at two-thousand four-hundred dollars. As she expected to sell it for a little more than four-thousand, this was an excellent deal. She grabbed Valerie's hand excitedly as her heart performed a tap-dance across her diaphragm.

She'd only just begun.

Later on, after she'd bid on the early nineteenth-century wardrobe, the Federico Munari Velvet Curved Sofa, the French nineteenth-century commode, the mid-century five-dresser drawer, and the French country-style chest, Brittany handed the baton to Valerie to let her bid on whatever she pleased.

Valerie's eyes were alight with excitement when, three items later, an absolutely gorgeous mahogany Chinese Chippendale desk was wheeled out. She nudged her mother and whispered, "That's the one."

Brittany whispered, "Yes. It'll fit the place perfectly. Go for it."

Valerie operated like a well-oiled machine. She pushed her bids further, but never too far, and eventually out-bid an antique dealer from Manhattan. She got the piece for just a little over seven-hundred, which was a steal for such a thing.

At seven-thirty, the auction had an intermission for dinner and drinks. Brittany always loved this portion, gossiping with the other buyers and sellers, admitting defeat against the ones who'd nabbed the pieces you wanted, and talking about the state of the antique industry these days. Several people Brittany had known for years came up to them to congratulate Valerie on her tremendous work in the bidding war for the Chippendale, and, instead of blush, as Brittany might have at that age, Valerie simply thanked them and said she learned it all from the best.

"Your mother is the best," one older gentleman named Chester affirmed. "She's been beating me out of my top choices for years. She's got a sharp eye for detail." He then turned toward Brittany to add, "I heard through the grapevine that you planned to expand your collection. Not such a surprise to find you here at Lake George..."

"I used to share the space with a coffee shop," Brittany affirmed. "But now, I've incorporated the coffee shop within the store and am trying to fill the space around it. It's a difficult task, but I think the space is finally coming together. And you know me. There's nothing I like more than buying these gorgeous pieces from the past."

"It's something we share, Mrs. Radley," Chester affirmed.

"Just call me Brittany, Chester," Brittany returned, smiling to let him know it wasn't any trouble. "My husband has nothing at all to do with my business."

"Very well then," Chester said, dropping his hand down to shake both Brittany and Valerie's hands. "I look forward to seeing you both around the circuit."

The auction finally drew to a close around ten-fifteen that night. Brittany ensured her items were positioned in the corner of the warehouse, each labeled with her name and the name of the driver she'd hired to collect them. On top of one of the boxes, she left a large box of homemade brownies and a note of thanks. She'd already paid the driver one-half of the large amount it cost to get the items from Upstate New York back to Bar Harbor, but the extra brownie touch ensured they'd get there in a safe manner. At least, this is what she'd told herself when she'd slaved away, baking them two nights before their departure.

Back at the hotel, Brittany and Valerie changed into their pajamas and talked excitedly about the items they'd purchased at the auction, each of which seemed entirely unique, apt to bring in remarkable revenue. They also spoke poetically about how they could arrange the space with the new items, drawing visitors in off the streets with the daydreamy array of old-world items.

"And it'll be tourist season before we know it," Valerie affirmed. "I cannot wait to see how they react..."

"I guess that means I can count on you for another summer of work?" Brittany asked.

"Are you kidding? I'm involved, now, Mom," Valerie affirmed.

It tugged on Brittany's heartstrings, knowing that by August or September, Valerie would be off somewhere, attending college, meeting friends, finding herself. Perhaps she'd do that in Chicago or New York or Paris or Beijing. Regardless of where she chose, it would be miles away from Brittany and Bar Harbor Antiques.

It was important to treasure every moment before it drifted away.

Chapter Eight

Valerie and Brittany spent the next morning at a nearby brunch place, eating savory biscuits slathered with honey and speckled with melted butter, bacon that oozed grease, bright yellow fried eggs, and yogurt topped with raspberries and blueberries. Brittany received a message that the driver had already passed the state line between New York and Vermont, headed back toward their Bar Harbor home, and she lifted a hand to high-five her daughter, who returned it.

"Guess we'll get back later tonight?" Valerie suggested, scooping three blueberries into a yogurt-laden spoon.

"I don't know..." Brittany eyed her daughter mischievously, then said, "I had this idea that we'd hit up a few of the schools you were thinking about in this area. Vermont... University of Maine..."

Valerie's jaw dropped. "What? What do you mean?"

"You know... Just park the SUV nearby and roam the campus, see what it feels to be one of the students."

"I don't know." Valerie's eyes were stormy with what Brittany could only assume was fear.

"It's not like anyone is going to make you take a test," Brittany pointed out. "Not that you wouldn't ace it. Your SAT score was in the top five of everyone in your graduating class."

"Nobody cares what your SAT score is anymore."

Brittany placed her fork against the edge of her plate, tilted her head, and tried to catch Valerie's eye. Valerie stared down at the round orb of her fried egg as though she studied it.

"What is it about college, Val? Why haven't you picked where you want to go?"

Valerie shrugged. "I just can't picture it yet. It seems like this whole other life that somebody else is supposed to live, not me."

Brittany nodded. "I think I can understand that. Probably that's partially why your brother hasn't picked a place yet."

"He seems happy as a lobster fisherman," Valerie countered.

"Yes, but I just don't know how long that happiness lasts," Brittany told her. "If you don't have a dream or a vision for yourself..."

"Maybe dreams and visions aren't necessary," Valerie tried.

Brittany could feel Conner's negativity within Valerie's words. Brittany lowered her eyebrows and gestured toward the back country roads, where they'd gone yesterday to purchase some of the most beautifully designed pieces Brittany had ever seen up close.

"Didn't you feel something yesterday? Some brightness? Optimism? Anything?"

Valerie nodded subtly.

"You feel that because I created this world," Brittany said, "Based on my dream. My vision. Do not think for a second that anything is too silly to dream up. Do not let your father's cynicism dig into you."

Silence fell across the table. Valerie nodded, her eyes still on that now-cold fried egg. Brittany nibbled at the edge of a slice of bacon, wondering about her daughter, about her sincere brilliance alongside her lack of confidence. No prom date. No college decision. No dreams.

"I guess it won't hurt to just go to the University of Vermont. Just to see it," Valerie finally offered, her eyelashes flickering skyward. "Especially this time of year."

* * *

The University of Vermont was located in Burlington, Vermont. According to the brochure, it was opened in 1781 and was known as a public Ivy school and sat on four hundred and sixty acres of beautiful land between the Adirondack and Green Mountains.

Although it was Sunday and quite busy near the campus, Brittany managed to find a two-hour parking spot for only three dollars an hour. As she paid the meter with her card, Valerie crossed her arms tightly over her chest and blinked out toward the old-world buildings, which seemed to have been taken directly from a painting.

"Look at that. It's coming alive with spring." Brittany aligned herself with her daughter as they breezed toward the edge of campus, which was lined with the bursting first shots of flowers. Students breezed past, wearing ridiculous boots and leggings and enormous North Face winter jackets, which made them look like amorphous cartoon characters. Laughter rang out from groups of them, which made Valerie's face twist with confusion and intrigue.

Perhaps, Valerie thought she would laugh like that with a group of newly-discovered girlfriends at this very campus.

"We should really hit the library today..." Brittany tried, blushing through her smile. "I have a huge paper due on

Wednesday. And didn't you say you have a test with Peterson?"

Valerie skipped a beat, analyzing her mother before playing along. "Don't remind me. And you know how awful the coffee is at the library."

"Is it?" Brittany wagged her eyebrows playfully, whispering, "Let's go check it out."

Together, they hustled across the campus to discover the Billings Memorial Library, which looked more like a medieval castle than anything else. They hurried through the double-wide doors to discover a glorious and shining all-wood interior, with students in sweatshirts seated at the tables, their elbows smashed against the antique tables.

"This place is a dream, Valerie." Brittany breathed, gripping her daughter's hand. "Imagine the life you could have here."

For the first time, hope beamed out from Valerie's eyes. She watched the students, leaning forward to try to catch their whispered words, the intensity of their study-mission. Brittany hopped toward the line behind the coffee cart, where she purchased two coffees that Valerie rated as "B or B+," which wasn't too bad in terms of coffee cart coffee.

When Brittany left to use the bathroom for no longer than five minutes, she returned to find her eighteen-year-old daughter in conversation with a pimply but cute college student, a guy with a big University of Vermont sweatshirt and overly-white tennis shoes who complained about his current coarse load and considered dropping all his classes and running off to Europe, like his brother had.

Brittany hung back, listening to Valerie as she pretended to be a University of Vermont student.

"I mean, Europe's great, obviously," she answered. "But you can do that any time you want. Imagine having to come back to college later on as an older student? It wouldn't be as fun, would it?"

The student groaned inwardly. "That's what I keep coming back to, too. I don't know." He slid his fingers through his hair, giving Valerie one of those adorable looks only men could give women. He'd drummed up the courage to talk to her. But what would happen next?

"I don't know. But do you like it? Want to exchange numbers? I might need another pep talk about staying in school," the guy told Valerie.

Brittany's heart leaped into her throat. She ducked behind another group of people, her hand clutched tightly around her coffee cup. Between the students, she watched Valerie use a pen and notepad to write down her information. She passed it over to the male student, who nodded in apparent disbelief before saying, "I'll see you around."

Valerie rushed for the double-wide door, turning her head just so to catch her mother's eye. Brittany knew to go along with the ruse. She walked evenly toward the glittering sunlight of this perfect April afternoon, where she found her daughter's face lifted, a look of bliss caught across her cheeks.

"Hey stranger," Brittany teased.

Valerie gave her a sharp yet playful look. "Not another word..."

"Come on! What did you give him?" Brittany asked as they sauntered across campus, both feeling, in their own way, that they owned the place. "You couldn't have given him your own information."

"Nah. I gave them the phone number of the ice cream place on Main Street in Bar Harbor," Valerie replied with a mischievous laugh.

"The one on that big sign?" Brittany asked.

"Yeah. I've seen it probably forty-thousand times in my life," Valerie said. "I have it memorized."

"What's that guy going to do when he tries to call you and gets just an ice cream parlor two states away?"

Valerie shrugged. "Not really my problem, is it?"

Brittany cackled. "Poor guy. Actually, poor all guys you'll meet in college."

"I wouldn't be here for them," Valerie offered thoughtfully, shoving her hands in her pockets. "I would be here for me."

"With the added benefit of flirting with the occasional cute boy..." Brittany tried.

Valerie's cheeks ballooned with red blotches. Only the corners of her mouth curved into a smile. Brittany traced her hand across Valerie's shoulder and said, "All right. I'll stop teasing you. Shall we head off to the next stop?"

Valerie and Brittany drove next to Durham, New Hampshire, where the University of New Hampshire was located. After they parked, Brittany read online that this university was apparently a "good value" school, which meant that its graduates generally went on to earn decent money and have worthwhile careers.

"How can they tell if someone's career is worthwhile?" Valerie asked with a sneaky smile. "What does that even mean?"

"Probably they ask if their careers are fulfilling in some way," Brittany tried. "I guess, at the end of the day, what you do for money is how you spend around forty to fifty hours of your week. You're going to want to like it."

"That's true."

Valerie and Brittany toured the campus quickly before jumping into a place called Hop + Grind for dinner. While there, Brittany booked a hotel room there in Durham, as she felt too exhausted to take them the rest of the way back to Bar Harbor that night.

"It's just four hours," Brittany recited as she dipped a French fry through a blotch of mayonnaise on the plate between them. "We could get up around seven, have a decent breakfast, then be back around one?"

"You're not planning on opening the shop?" Valerie asked.

"No. But that reminds me..." Brittany grabbed her phone to check on the drop-off of the recently-purchased antiques.

BRITTANY: Hey Gabe! Are you still good to come to the warehouse to oversee the arrival of the new inventory?

GABE: I just got a message from the driver a few minutes ago saying he's ten minutes away. I'm waiting outside the warehouse door now.

GABE: I can't wait to see the beautiful pieces you picked out!

"Are you worried?" Valerie asked, lifting her cheeseburger tentatively.

"No, not really. I just want to make sure everything gets there in one piece," Brittany answered. "Thousands and thousands of dollars worth of inventory, crossing multiple state lines..."

"I can't believe you managed to sleep last night," Valerie teased.

"Yeah, yeah. I'll try to forget about it," Brittany countered. "Gabe will let me know if there are any problems."

"Eat up," Valerie instructed. "And tonight, I think we should watch a movie in the hotel. Something to keep your mind off of this delivery and my mind off of this difficult college decision."

Around two hours later, just as Brittany and Valerie began watching *Notting Hill* on the hotel television, Gabe sent several photographs from the inside of the warehouse, proof that the inventory had been delivered safely and positioned appropriately around the space.

GABE: It took forever for them to unload all that heavy furniture, poor guys.

GABE: But I made sure they treated it with the utmost care.

BRITTANY: I knew I could count on you, Gabe. Thanks a bunch.

* * *

The following afternoon, Brittany and Valerie reached Bar Harbor at twelve-forty-seven, both over-sugared, over-salted, and over-caffeinated. For multiple hours, they'd debated the pros and cons of both Vermont and New Hampshire alongside what they remembered from their trip to the University of Maine. So far, the University of Vermont came out on top, although Valerie's opinion seemed malleable, easily changed from hour to hour.

"Let me just check on those beauties," Brittany said as she eased through downtown, passing by the ice cream place that Valerie had used for phone number purposes, the hotel where Casey's husband, Grant, had hid out, waiting for her to wise up about their marriage, and the Italian restaurant where, once upon a time, Conner had asked Brittany to marry him.

Bar Harbor surged with memories she would never forget.

But it would always remain home.

Brittany entered the back alley behind Bar Harbor Antiques, parked alongside the large warehouse, and jumped out of the SUV. Valerie got out with her, stretching her arms above her head until they crackled.

"Okay. What about we check out the inventory, grab some lunch from the diner, and then start to figure out the strategy for the week ahead?" Brittany began excitedly, walking with purpose toward the warehouse door.

"Our eating adventures are never finished!" Valerie cried.

Brittany laughed, jangling her keys from her pocket and finding the two warehouse ones, one for the deadbolt and one for the knob. With the deadbolt cracked open, she slowly eased the doorknob to the right and stepped through the shadows of the warehouse, just as she'd done nearly every day for the previous twenty-five years.

But when she entered the warehouse space itself, she found it nearly empty.

Brittany's heart dropped into her belly like a stone. She couldn't scream; her tongue felt heavy, and it was as though her mouth was filled with cotton balls.

Valerie ambled in behind Brittany, chatting words that Brittany couldn't understand. It was as though she'd lost all comprehension of English.

Finally, Valerie stopped dead beside her mother, there in the empty space.

The warehouse felt literally hollow, with only some of the desks and couches from the fifties and sixties still stuffed in the corner, inventory Brittany had had waiting around for almost three years.

"Um... Mom?" Valerie breathed, her voice wavering. "Where is all our stuff?"

Chapter Nine

L unch date.

Why in the world had Brad thought that was a good idea? There was a real awkwardness to a lunch date, or at least, this was what he currently learned as he tried to eat a sandwich that fell apart between his hands, listening intently, or half-intently, to the school teacher that his cop friends had set him up with. The sunlight was too bright through the floor-to-ceiling window of the diner. Her lipstick stained her teeth and Brad didn't know how to tell her. When she asked him a question, the diner waitress dropped a huge platter of salads and soups across the floor, casting one-half of the diner in stinky misery.

"Oh no." The teacher, whose name was Stacy, looked on the verge of leaping up to help.

Brad wanted to tell her to do it. *Get up from the table. Go over there. Stop this painful conversation in its tracks.*

"Gosh, I just feel so bad for them," Stacy breathed, dabbing her napkin across her lower lip and again missing the large dash of lipstick on her teeth. "I worked as a waitress in college. I still have dreams that cause more stress than my present life. And I'm a teacher! My entire life is stress, but I'm sure I don't have to tell you about stress. You're a cop."

Was this how people talked to one another? This was Brad's first first-date in over three years. Had he opted for a dinner date, perhaps they could have at least eased into conversation with a glass of wine or two and a big bowl of garlic bread. He'd already asked Stacy what grade she taught in school; he'd already asked when she'd moved to Bar Harbor and where she'd gone to college. He wasn't even sure if she'd said the University of Maine or the University of Maryland anymore and was terrified to get it wrong.

"Did you ever work as one?"

"As what?" Brad asked, realizing he'd lost the train of the conversation.

"As a waiter," Stacy returned, clearly annoyed.

"Oh. Yeah. I mean, no. I was never. A waiter."

Really? You just had to shove your foot in your mouth! Now, she'll more than likely tell my buddies how much of an arse she thinks I am or how rude I was to her.

Brad's phone buzzed in his pocket. He reached for it, dropping it on the table between them to find a message from another cop named Walter.

WALTER: Hey. We got a robbery downtown at Bar Harbor Antiques.

Brad's heart surged with surprise. He lifted his chin to meet Stacy's gaze, then dropped his eyes back to the message. Brittany Keating Radley owned Bar Harbor Antiques. Brittany Keating, that beautiful woman he'd encountered over in Lewiston all those months ago. That was before he'd heard his colleagues had had to escort her emotionally abusive husband out of the house, before the gossip around their divorce and Conner Radley's disappearance. Before so much.

Had Brad thought once or twice about stopping into Bar

Harbor Antiques to say hello? He had. But fear had gotten the better of him. That, and embarrassment. He didn't want Brittany to think he was "after" her after their brief flirtation in Lewiston. He was out of practice, anyway. Maybe it hadn't been a flirtation at all.

"What's going on?" Stacy asked, her tone light, as though she asked about the weather instead. She shifted her straw around in her water glass, clinking it through the ice.

"I'm really sorry, Stacy," Brad apologized as he leaped to his feet. "There's been a robbery. I have to cut this short."

"A robbery, huh?" Stacy's eyes brightened at the first sound of gossip. "Who was it?"

"I can't share that information with you," Brad told her, reaching into his wallet to tug out a twenty-dollar bill. "Think this covers it?"

"You've hardly touched your sandwich," Stacy pointed out.

"You should have it. If you want." He paused, trying to come up with something to say, something that would wrap this up with a neat bow. "It was nice to meet you."

The waitresses had only just begun to clean up the salad and soup from the diner floor. Brad hustled around some booths and rushed down the aisle for the front door, even as one of the waitresses demanded what he was doing. Once outside beneath the glistening April sky, Brad turned south on Main Street and headed toward Bar Harbor Antiques, which was a little more than a quarter-mile away.

Downtown Bar Harbor bustled with spring-time revelers, their faces lifted toward the Maine sunshine and their words hopeful for an approaching summer in New England. Brad weaved around them as quickly as he could, probably doubling the time it should have taken him to get there, and stopped directly in front of Bar Harbor Antiques, his hands wrapped around his knees as he gasped for air. For most of his adult life, he'd run five miles three days per week. But now, with his fiftieth birthday peeking around the corner, he noticed a slight shift in his athleticism. One of the downfalls of getting older, but he always took it in stride.

"There he is." Walter, dressed in his uniform, stepped around the side of his police car and gestured for Brad to approach. From this side of Bar Harbor Antiques, Brad couldn't make out the entrance to the warehouse, and the interior of the shop itself was dark and shadowed.

"Hey, there. What happened?" Brad asked.

"First off, Brad, I gotta apologize," Walter began. "The guys at the office just reminded me that you're off today. On a date with that school teacher."

"Don't worry about it," Brad said with a wave of his hand.

"But Brad, this was your first date in who knows how long..." Walter reminded him.

"Walter! My allegiance is to the city of Bar Harbor. Not my dating life."

Walter hesitated, as though he wanted to argue, but then he shifted his head toward the antique shop and said, "Brittany Keating left town this weekend for an antique auction in New York State. She paid a moving company to bring a massive amount of antiques from New York to Maine. Every piece was accounted for last evening during drop-off, but when Brittany Keating arrived back from out-of-state this afternoon, she found the warehouse essentially empty."

"Jesus..." Brad whispered. "Where's Britt—I mean, where's Ms. Keating?"

"She's in the shop," Walter replied, palming the back of his neck as he continued to look around the empty warehouse.

Brad bustled forward, his head buzzing with intrigue. Who on earth could have stolen so much merchandise in a single night? And why had they targeted Brittany Keating? Had someone tipped them off that she'd had so many expensive articles shipped to Bar Harbor from New York?

The front door of Bar Harbor Antiques was open, and the bell jangled, reminiscent of Christmas, as Brad stepped through. Before him on an antique couch sat Brittany Keating, her daughter Valerie, and a man in his twenties, who pressed a Kleenex against the edge of his eye as his stomach bounced with sorrowful hiccups.

"Hi." Brad was grateful that he could trust his voice to be both commanding and calm in even the most dire of situations. His eyes connected with Brittany's as she stood. It looked as though she'd been crying but had recently forced herself to stop. She seemed the sort of woman to realize when the tears were enough.

"Brad. It's good to see you again." Brittany reached out to shake his hand formally.

"How are you three holding up?" Brad asked, trying to ignore the shiver that went up and down his spine as Brittany's hand slid against his. This wasn't the time for emotions.

"It's been a whirlwind," Brittany explained timidly. "Gabe here met the truck last night while Valerie and I were still in New Hampshire."

"Everything was accounted for," Gabe shot out. "I took pictures of everything, just like Brittany told me to. I can show you the documents, which both the driver and I signed."

Gabe grabbed the documents from the side table beside him and passed them to Brad, who nodded formally at the two signatures along with the date and time. Brad knew, of course, that signatures could be forged— that pen and paper mattered, but only so far.

Brittany seemed to sense his hesitance. She grabbed her phone and went through the images that Gabe had sent the previous night, all of which were time-stamped. This didn't totally clear Gabe from involvement in the crime, but it did prove that the inventory had been at the warehouse at that specific time.

"I'm going to need a record of all of this," Brad informed them. "Along with statements from all of you about the past few days."

"Of course," Brittany replied. "Anything you need."

Brad met with Gabe first, who struggled to get through his report, as he seemed about to burst into tears at any moment. "Brittany should have been able to trust me with this," he whispered, staring out the window of Brittany's back office, where Brad conducted the interviews. "But I feel like I failed her somehow. Like maybe I made some kind of mistake."

Later, Brittany affirmed that she'd had to unlock both the bolt and the door upon her arrival to the warehouse. "That doesn't necessarily mean that whoever opened it didn't have a key. But why would they lock up again after stealing all my belongings? Was it for some kind of dramatic effect?"

Brad agreed that it seemed rather silly to bother to do that. "And what about CCTV footage? Anything?"

"The camera was destroyed," Brittany announced. "We really should have bought more, put them in hidden locations. Hindsight is twenty-twenty, I suppose."

Brad noticed, mid-way through their conversation, that Brittany wore a particularly riveting perfume, one that made him slightly more distracted than he wanted to be. Trying to shove that out of his mind, he asked Brittany to walk him through the steps of Saturday's auction, Sunday's college visits, and finally, her and Valerie's arrival at the warehouse. Brittany did, giving him mostly details that didn't matter to the investigation. Brad found himself hanging on every word, even the most boring, in ways he hadn't managed with Stacy earlier.

Brittany stuttered as she finally added, "I don't know how anyone could have known this... But my insurance hadn't yet been covered for the extra amount of inventory. I had two weeks. Two weeks before the insurance came through..."

Suddenly, her eyes filled with tears as she dropped her chin toward her chest. Brad wanted to reach out and take her hand but held himself back.

"I'm sorry for the question, Brittany. But is there a possibility that your ex-husband knew about your lack of insurance?" Brad asked.

Brittany sniffled. "Nobody really knew. Not even Gabe. Not even my daughter. It was a shameful thing, something I didn't want to admit to anyone."

Brad's throat tightened. "Do you think there's a possibility that anyone at the auction had something to do with this?"

"I don't know. The antique community is competitive, but it's not cruel. I bought those pieces fair and square. Anyone involved in the auction would have respected that."

Silence swelled between them. Brad remembered again what his colleagues had said about Conner Radley, about the way he'd fought tooth-and-nail as they'd dragged him out of his own home. Had this woman really lived with that monster for all those years?

Brad asked the following question with his most tender, softest tone.

"Even if he didn't know about the insurance, do you think it's possible your ex-husband still had a hand in the robbery?"

Brittany bowed her head again, speaking to the ground. "I think there's a definite possibility. But I don't know how he could have operated something like this, something on such a grand scale. That said, one thing you can count on is Conner Radley's anger. And since he left Bar Harbor, he's been terribly quiet. Maybe he felt it was time to destroy me."

Chapter Ten

That night, Brittany sat at the kitchen table, half a bottle of wine deep, her hair tied up in a high ponytail and her body swaddled in sweats. Valerie had recently retreated upstairs, and now, her voice was muffled and inarticulate as she talked with a girlfriend on the phone. Brittany had been initially grateful for the moment of solitude until the true terror of what had happened and the depths of her mistake crept up on her, making her sizzle in despair.

For dinner, Brittany and Valerie had baked frozen pizzas in the oven and crunched on the non-nutritional food, staring at their phones. Sometimes, they said things like, *"I hope Gabe is okay,"* or, *"The antique network has been alerted of the robbery,"* or, *"Do you want a brownie?"* But mostly, they remained somber and silent, two barely-moveable zombies stewing in their own defeat.

With Valerie upstairs, Brittany decided to do something she'd never imagined she would.

She lifted her phone, dialed Conner's phone number, and pressed the phone to her ear. It rang out, first once, then twice, then five more times. Conner's voice filled her ear with the voicemail message, which said:

"Hi. You've reached Conner Radley. I can't come to the phone right now, but please leave your name and your purpose for calling at the beep."

The voice sent sinister shivers up and down Brittany's spine. She nearly threw the phone against the wall. After a moment, she forced herself to inhale as much air into her lungs as she could, then dialed the number again. She could feel Conner Radley out there, lurking around his phone, watching her call.

Brittany technically still knew him better than anyone. If she asked him, *"Hey, Conner, did you have a hand in stealing my inventory?"* she knew that the tone of his answer would tell her everything she needed to know, that slippery snake.

After several more attempts to call her ex-husband, Brittany's divorce lawyer, Mary, called her.

"Hey, there." Mary's tone was difficult to read.

"Hi..."

Mary heaved a sigh. "I just got a call from Conner's lawyer saying that you've been obsessively calling him, which goes against the bounds of the agreement we have with him?"

Brittany groaned. "Mary, you must have heard what happened this afternoon."

"I did, Brittany. I'm so sorry. I don't even know what to say."

"I feel like he had something to do with it," Brittany admitted. "And I need to ask him point-blank to hear his answer."

"Brittany..." Mary's voice crackled with sorrow. "It just can't work like that. I'm sorry."

Brittany got off the phone shortly thereafter, truly troubled that Conner had gone out of his way to call his lawyer about her rather than answer her himself. *Was he a coward? Or was he just trying to mess with her?* Both options seemed plausible.

Brittany refilled her wine glass and contemplated what to do with herself for the rest of the night. It was clear she wouldn't get much sleep.

There was a knock at the front door. Brittany nearly leaped out of her skin, suddenly conscious of the subtle ways she'd grown fearful since their return to Bar Harbor just that afternoon. The rules of the world had changed.

Another knock. Brittany puffed out her cheeks and walked with purpose toward the front door, prepared to tell any neighbors or friends that she wasn't up for a hang-out. But when she opened the door, she discovered none other than Heather and Nicole Harvey before her, touting bottles of wine and fancy bars of chocolate.

"Thank goodness you're here," Brittany told them with a sigh. "I was terrified I was going to run out of wine."

Together, Heather and Nicole sat across from Brittany at the kitchen table and listened to Brittany's tale of woe.

"The CCTV camera was broken?" Nicole demanded, shocked.

"The plastic was all over the floor," Brittany affirmed. "I just received word from the police officer on the case, Brad Wethers, that they discovered a broken window in the back, which means that it's possible that whoever broke in, broke in through that window, opened the garage doors, loaded everything onto trucks in just a few hours, closed the garage door and sped out of sight. But so far, they haven't discovered any fingerprints. There's nothing concrete to go on."

"Only your suspicion that Conner behind this," Heather interjected.

"It was obviously Conner," Nicole added. "Who else could it have been?"

"I don't know how I could ever prove that," Brittany offered. "And I don't know how he would have known this was the perfect time, either. My insurance wasn't slated to come through for another two weeks. Most of the stuff I bought over the weekend isn't covered, which means I lost thirty-two thousand dollars of inventory, which I'd slated for over ninety grand in revenue."

"Oh my God," Heather breathed.

"Yeah." Brittany groaned as she added, "It's actually the first time I've said that number out loud. And I think if I say it again, I'll have a heart attack."

The three women were silent for nearly a full minute as they took in the gravity of the situation. Upstairs, Valerie's voice murmured on.

"What would one do with all that stolen inventory?" Nicole finally asked.

"It's difficult to say," Brittany offered. "I guess they could sell it privately via Craigslist or social media. That would make it really difficult to track. That said, if they're stupid and they bring some of the pieces to auctions across New England, it's possible to track some of that stuff down."

"How would we do that?" Nicole demanded. "It's not realistic to drive to every single auction."

"No. It's not. But I have all the official documentation of ownership for the antiques I purchased over the weekend. It might take a lifetime, but I'd need to take photographs of the documents and send them across the antique circuit across New England to every person in charge of every single auction. Perhaps that way, someone might flag a piece and alert me that it's there."

"Then we could drive there and track the person down!" Heather cried.

"Maybe. Or maybe that person got it off of someone else... This world is a slippery one," Brittany breathed. "That was always something I liked about it, that these antiques are passed from one person to another through history. But just now, it makes things very messy for me."

"Is there a way we can help you reach out to all these antique auctioneers?" Heather asked.

Brittany's eyes widened with surprise. "Like I said. It'll take many, many hours to sort through everything."

"Yeah, but Brittany. This is your livelihood. Someone stole from you. And we want to track them down," Nicole affirmed. "Let us help you. We've set aside the time."

Brittany was so overwhelmed that she nearly burst into tears all over again. Her eyes closed, she raised a glass of wine to her lips, sipped it, and said, "When the Harvey Sisters came into my life last year, I couldn't have envisioned what generous gifts they were from the universe. You've been by my side through thick and thin. And this— this is my darkest moment of all. Thank you."

Together, Nicole, Heather, and Brittany drank through a bottle of wine and made up a plan for the following several days, with each woman in charge of a set number of antiques and a set number of auctioneers. It was probably impossible to reach everyone, and Brittany thought they were probably foolish to try. Still, it was the only plan they had so far. She had to believe that maybe, their actions could make a difference. She had to believe she could get some of her pieces back.

Chapter Eleven

T he Bar Harbor police department wasn't exactly
accustomed to real criminal activity. Bar Harbor was
ordinarily a sleepy town, with only the occasional
disorderly conduct or drunk driving activity, plus a bit of extortion and, sometimes, a runaway teenager. With this enormous
robbery on their hands, Brad Wethers found himself taking the
reins, sending colleagues to interview neighbors of Bar Harbor
Antiques about any activity they might have seen around the
shop, and taking a very detailed account of every single thing
Gabe, Valerie, and Brittany had told him the previous
afternoon.

Now, Brad dialed the truck company who'd been in charge
of delivering Brittany's inventory Sunday night. After two
rings, a very cheerful secretary greeted him, asking what she
could do. When Brad explained he needed to speak with the
truck driver who'd driven a large load of antiques to Bar Harbor
on Sunday night, she said that he was out on another delivery
but would be available the following morning. Brad asked for a
cell phone, anything to reach the man earlier, but the secretary

explained that their company prided itself on healthy work hours and commitment to family time after employees clocked out. Brad couldn't scoff at that, he supposed, no matter how much he wanted to.

"How did it go with Stacy yesterday?" A colleague marched past, knocking his knuckles across Brad's desk.

Truth be told, Brad had almost forgotten about Stacy. He couldn't have picked her out of a line-up, which was saying something, as Brad normally prided himself on having a photographic memory.

"She's a nice woman," Brad tried. *Wasn't that something else you were meant to say?*

"Did she tell you about all the marathons she runs? I figured, you know, you like to run, she likes to run..."

"We had so much other stuff to talk about that it didn't even come up," Brad lied.

"That's such fantastic news! You really deserve someone, Brad."

That night, Brad ate a roast beef sandwich from a fast-food restaurant and watched television from his armchair. It wasn't exactly a sad sight— after all, he'd worked a hard day and needed sustenance for crying out loud. Was Stacy the kind of woman who might have cooked him a big three-course meal, asked him about his day, and slowly coaxed him into a night of some cozy bed snuggling? Maybe. Maybe that's what existed behind all those decisions to fall in love. Maybe Brad just wasn't up for it.

After drinking a beer, Brad collected his cell phone and blinked at Stacy's name, trying to drum up the courage to ask her out again.

Sorry for running out like that.

I'm not normally like that...

Hi, Stacy! Care to try again?

But none of it seemed honest. He struggled to remember

why he'd agreed to the date in the first place. Was it because his colleagues all felt bad for him? Did he want to uphold some sense of decency in the community? Was he tired of his sister calling him every weekend and asking him if he ever planned to try again? Maybe.

Brad fell asleep just past nine in the evening and awoke at five-thirty sharp to head out on a chilly run across the town, scooping into Acadia National Park and then looping back to his little house. When he reached his front stoop, his smart watch told him he'd run across seven miles, which wasn't so bad, was it? He then drank a protein smoothie, washed himself clean in the shower, and found himself back at the police station by eight o'clock, prepared to dial the truck driver who'd made Brittany's delivery the Sunday before.

This time, the driver was available.

"Hi, there. My name is Brad Wethers, and I work on the police force in Bar Harbor, Maine," Brad began, grateful that his voice was both confident and easygoing at once.

"Hi, Brad Wethers from Bar Harbor," the driver echoed. "How can I be of service?"

"I was wondering if I could ask you about the delivery you made Sunday evening for a woman named Brittany Keating," Brad continued.

"Gosh, yeah. My back sure remembers some of those antiques. My wife has me doing yoga these days to try to stretch it out after those big hauls. But truth be told, I'm in my sixties, now. I shouldn't be lifting so much. It's high time for me to admit that to myself, so I guess I'll start with admitting it to you."

Brad found his heart swelling with genuine happiness. He liked this man, liked the tone of his voice and the self-deprecating way he spoke about himself. Brad was too good a cop to think that these factors made any person "innocent," per se. But if Brad's gut instinct had anything to do with it, it would say—this man was not involved in the robbery.

Brad went on to explain that Brittany's antiques had been stolen that night, that the CCTV camera had been smashed, and that they needed to collect all known evidence prior to the incident. The truck driver was gobsmacked with the news.

"You're kidding. All that beautiful furniture! It's not like I know two things about French or Italian design from the eighteenth century, mind you, but when Brittany explained some of the personal details of the pieces, I could really feel how important they were. That they'd lived through war and famine and boat rides across the Atlantic, just to get over to that auction in New York State."

Brad asked the man to give him a detailed explanation of the ride from Lake George back to Bar Harbor. The man told him more than Brad needed— that he'd gotten an oil change before the trip, that he'd made four stops for food and bathroom breaks, and that he'd run into a good deal of traffic in New Hampshire of all places, which was a rare thing.

"My buddy Mike helped me with the unloading when we arrived in Bar Harbor," the driver continued. "That young man Gabe checked us in and, I believe, took some photographs to send over to Brittany. After that, Mike and I checked into a nearby hotel and left Bar Harbor around eight that Monday morning. We were back in New York by the afternoon."

"And you didn't interact with anyone besides Gabe and Mike after you left New York State Sunday morning?" Brad asked.

"No one except gas station clerks and restaurant waitresses," the driver told him. "It seemed like a routine job up until now. I really hope you get a sense of what happened. Brittany doesn't deserve this."

"No. She doesn't."

Throughout the call, the driver agreed to send Brad all

evidence of his trek across New England, including receipts that proved his location at the approximate time he'd said. "I know how these things go," the driver explained. "I'd just prefer to get out in front of this one and blot out my name."

Brad worked tirelessly over the next eight hours, both on Brittany's case and a few others (ones that didn't exactly illuminate his police mind but were necessary for the betterment of Bar Harbor at-large). He also attempted to reach out to Conner Radley's divorce lawyer, who was apparently the only line of communication to Conner Radley himself. After two attempts, Brad left his name, number, and email address. By three p.m., Conner's lawyer had responded via email to say:

Dear Officer Wethers,

Conner Radley has made the decision to stay as far away from his wife's life as possible and maintains a residence outside the city of Bar Harbor. He declines to be interviewed at this time. If you have reason to take him into custody for an in-person interview, that's another story, but I have a hunch that your evidence for such a thing is negligent.

Annoyed, Brad rolled his eyes and clicked out of the email. Speaking through lawyers was always a dragged-out attempt to reach any sort of conclusion. The best was to surprise a potential criminal and hope he gave something away. But with Conner out there somewhere, in a "residence outside the city of Bar Harbor," hope for that was minimal if non-existent.

By the time Brad clocked out at four-thirty, he found his stomach gurgling with hunger and another afternoon and evening stretched before him without any plan. Loneliness was like an illness he couldn't shake.

A little later, Brad found himself directing his police vehicle over to Brittany Keating's house, the place she'd purchased with her husband twenty years ago (according to the file about Conner Radley, which they had at the station). He hovered in his car for a good two minutes, the engine still purring, as he pondered what to do next. On the one hand, Brittany probably didn't need the stress of a police officer just showing up to her place like this. On the other, he wanted to let her know all he'd done for her case thus far— and ask her if she'd received any word from her ex-husband, who might have called to gloat.

After two police-worthy knocks on the door, Heather Harvey opened it with a bright smile, her ocean-blue eyes catching the late afternoon springtime light.

"Hello, Officer," she greeted him, her hand holding the door ajar.

Behind her, a large table had been set up directly in the living room, upon which were a number of manilla envelopes, file organizers, and stacks of yellowed papers. Brittany and Nicole hovered over the table, both in reading glasses, reading something intently. A MacBook glowed off to the left, a contrast to the old-world paper display.

"What can we do for you?" Heather asked finally.

"I wanted to stop by and chat for a little while about the case," Brad said hurriedly. "But I see you're all in the middle of something."

Brittany, seemingly finished with her read-through, finally lifted her eyes to meet his. Her smile was genuine, beautiful— nothing forced, like other women.

"Hello, Brad." She stepped around the table, opened the door wider, and gestured for him to enter. "My cousins graciously stepped in to help save me. We've been hard at work for a couple of days now."

"So much paperwork." Nicole groaned.

With Brad inside, Brittany closed the door, latching them all within the glowing warmth of her mid-century home.

Brad's eyes danced across the walls and the fireplace mantle, on the hunt for some sign of Conner Radley— a photograph of a once-happy family, anything. There were several photographs, all of Valerie and Thomas in various stages of growing up. Conner had been eliminated from exposed memory.

"How is the case going?" Brittany asked her hands on her hips.

Brad explained what he knew so far, based on interviews with Bar Harbor shop owners, the delivery truck driver, and various other potential leads. He tried to make it sound more than it was but soon found himself tracing the same details over and over. Brittany nodded, her brow furrowing. He then explained that he'd been in contact with her ex-husband's lawyer, but he'd been less-than-helpful.

"Welcome to the club," Brittany affirmed. "And I know that if we don't have any evidence against him, there's no way of tracking him down."

Silence swelled across the room.

Heather groaned inwardly and muttered, "Conner strikes again!"

"We don't actually know that for sure..." Nicole tried. "Innocent until proven guilty and all that."

"What are you up to here?" Brad asked.

Brittany brightened slightly as she explained their current task: arranging the paperwork of all the antiques she'd purchased the previous weekend, taking photographs, and reaching out to the antique auctioneer network across New England about the robbery.

"My hope is that if they see any of these items, they'll reach out to me before selling," Brittany explained. "Now that people are catching wind of the robbery, I'm receiving an outpouring of love from people in the field. Nobody has ever heard of a robbery on such a scale as this. They know what a blow it is to me. I'm just a little too embarrassed to explain that I didn't have my insurance set up to cover myself."

"It was only two weeks till it was set up, Brittany." Heather chimed in. "You should have been fine. Somebody knew. And that somebody was so obviously Con—"

"Let's stop saying his name," Nicole interjected. "I think it might bring bad luck."

"That's fine with me," Brittany said.

Brittany disappeared for a moment and returned with a mug of hot tea for Brad, which he accepted gratefully, even as his stomach rattled once more with hunger. Heather laughed outright, youthfully, and said that she and Luke were about to head out to grab a bite to eat.

"Sounds like you need a good meal, Officer Brad," she joked.

"Got a little carried away with work today and didn't eat properly," Brad affirmed. "But I have some soup at home."

"Soup? No way. You're not eating soup tonight," Heather told him. "Why don't you all come out to dinner with Luke and me? Nicole, you can call Evan, too, if you want. We can make it a get-together."

"I really shouldn't," Brad told them, trying to form an earnest expression on his face, one that illustrated just how much he had to do that night.

"Come on," Brittany tried to coax, her eyes dancing. "You're already working too hard on my case. Let's get out of this weird funk and go eat some grub."

Brad laughed good-naturedly, which was a sound he hadn't heard from his lips in quite some time. "Well, I'm off duty soon. I guess I don't have a choice, do I?"

"You really don't!" Heather called as she leaped for the coat rack, drawing her peacoat across her slender shoulders. "If we get there early, we can beat the Happy Hour rush. I have my eye on the appetizer platter."

Chapter Twelve

W as it a typical thing to go out to dinner with the police officer investigating the case of your business's robbery? Brittany wasn't sure this was a question she wanted to answer. But there he sat: Officer Brad Wethers, who now was tearing the edge of his napkin nervously as Heather ordered the appetizer platter, with its crunchy onion rings, its quesadillas, its mozzarella sticks, and its chicken wings. Heather then ordered a glass of rosé for herself, while Nicole opted for red wine. Brad hummed to himself, seemingly nervous, before he finally told the server, "I'll do an IPA." Brittany ordered an Aperol Spritz, a newfound delight that she'd heard was a specialty in Italy. Just after she ordered, her eyes met with Brad's, and a blush crept up her cheeks.

"I've never heard of that before," Brad said, his eyes alight with curiosity.

"Our Brittany's been changing her brand for the past few months," Heather said, folding her hands daintily across the table. "The new clothes. The spin classes. The rocking bod...

And now, the Italian cocktail. I mean, come on. Are you trying to prove you're better than the rest of us?"

Brittany's laugh twinkled across the restaurant even as embarrassment stewed in the base of her belly. "It's refreshing," she admitted with a shrug.

"Ciao Bella," Nicole teased, really laying into the Italian accent.

"Will you make them stop?" Brittany asked Brad. "Arrest them? Something?"

Luke appeared at the edge of the table, a bluster of nervous energy as he removed his coat and kissed Heather on the cheek.

"I hope I didn't miss anything?" Luke asked as he sat alongside Heather, burrowing himself over the drink menu. His eyes then scanned across the table, catching Officer Brad, who he nodded to. "I've seen you around, Officer, but I don't think we've ever been introduced."

"Brad. Brad Wethers." Brad raised a hand in greeting, his eyes nervous.

Brittany had no idea what Brad's private life was like. His fingers were bare, proof he was unmarried, and he seemed to fret over the smallest of words thrown his way, as though he wasn't often in social situations and wasn't sure what to make of them.

The server arrived back at the table with their drinks, including the round glass emitting the soft orange glow of Brittany's Aperol Spritz. Brad quickly took a drink, allowing the alcohol to wash away his anxiety and allowing a new sense of confidence to sweep over him. Brittany wanted to tell him to loosen up, that nobody was out to get him or make him look like a fool. But those words alone were like an attack.

"How's that beer?" Luke suddenly asked Brad.

Brad flashed a smile. "It's really good. I've always preferred bottled over draft."

"That's a good enough review for me," Luke said confidently. "I'll have that."

As they sipped through their drinks and chatted amicably, awaiting their food, Brad's shoulders eased back, his chin lifted. Heather and Nicole gabbed about the endless filing and organization that was required to potentially get Brittany's antiques back. Luke asked Brittany a series of questions about the disastrous weekend, including whether or not she'd had any contact with Conner. Brittany just sighed and said Conner refused to answer her calls, and his lawyer had essentially shoved both her and Officer Brad off with a "come back when you have proof" sentiment.

"I never liked that guy," Luke muttered, his nostrils flaring.

Brittany wanted to tell him that words like that made her feel about three inches small. They seemed to indicate that for all those years, everyone had just sat around, waiting for her to kick him out. Like she'd been this weak woman nobody had respected.

"Well, I think he's up to no good," Nicole affirmed. "You already said it was weird how quiet he's been since he went away."

"It is strange," Brittany said contemplatively. "Especially because the tiniest things used to mean a hurricane-level breakdown on his part. Like, if he'd envisioned something different for dinner than what I cooked. Or..."

"God. What. A. Narcissist," Heather shot out pointedly, puffing out her cheeks.

"It's not easy to see from within a relationship," Brad interjected simply, rushing to Brittany's aid.

Brittany eyed him curiously, grateful that he'd offered her this brief moment of empathy. Her throat tight, she whispered, "Thanks for saying that," just as Luke's drink arrived and Nicole edged them toward conversations that had nothing to do with Conner Radley.

As Evan Snow owned the restaurant, he soon breezed out of the back office, wearing a suit and a pair of shiny shoes and that same confident grin, one that only the Snow men could muster. A shiver rushed up and down Brittany's spine as he knelt to kiss Nicole on the cheek and wave a hand toward everyone else.

"Sit with us!" Nicole instructed. "We have so many appetizers coming. I know for a fact you've been working out too much. You have to feed those muscles."

"I don't know about that." But in a flash, he grabbed a chair from behind him, whipped it around, and sidled it between Nicole and Brittany.

As Evan slid in beside her, a server approached with a vodka-based cocktail and placed it directly in front of Evan without asking.

"Great service," Luke joked. "Are they scared of you?"

Evan laughed. "They shouldn't be. I just gave everyone a raise. Nicole convinced me to increase it to make up for the nights where they don't make much in tips. It makes total sense and it should encourage them to work a little harder."

Nicole beamed as she took a sip of wine. "I just don't think it's fair for servers to rely on their tips to offset their checks. We've implemented that system at Acadia Eatery, and I think there's a general air of goodwill— we're there for our employees, and they're there for us."

"Nice system," Brittany interjected, which drew Evan Snow's eyes toward hers. *What was this expression he gave her? Was it pride? Fear? Did he remember all those evenings he'd spent with her, Conner, and his wife, who'd died so tragically? Or were memories different for other people? Did they not stick in the same way?*

"Thank you," Evan said. He then bowed his head to add, "I was really horrified to hear what happened with Bar Harbor Antiques. I'm so sorry."

Brittany bristled. A strange and curious suspicion latched in the base of her stomach and seemed to grow up the sides of her belly. Was it possible that Evan knew something about the robbery, even outside of her close circles? Was it possible that he'd learned of the incident through Conner himself?

Trusting Evan Snow meant deleting an entire portion of her brain.

The appetizers arrive. Brittany's stomach twisted itself into knots. She gulped her Aperol Spritz as Evan talked about a redesign of one of his other restaurants, where they would soon experiment with a lobster menu. Brittany was reminded yet again of Conner, her lobster fisherman husband. *Was this his doing?*

When the server returned to ask about dinner orders, Heather, Nicole, Luke, and Evan ordered simply— salmon fillets drizzled with lemon, chunky mashed potatoes with plenty of butter, crab cakes, and seafood risotto. Brittany had forgotten to look at the menu for the main course. Apparently, Brad had, too.

"Sorry. Gosh. I don't know." Brad grabbed his menu again and flashed a finger toward a steak, which he wanted "medium-rare." Brittany said, "That sounds good," and passed her menu across the table, back toward the server. After the server left, she asked Brad, "Wait. What did you order?" And Brad laughed outright, sensing that her mind had been elsewhere.

"I got a steak. So did you."

"Oh gosh. No! I don't want that." Brittany dabbed her napkin across her forehead distractedly.

"You don't?" Brad's eyebrows jumped toward his hairline.

"I mean..." Brittany scrunched her nose and said, "I would really prefer the salmon."

Suddenly, Brad, who remained in his uniform, leaped to his feet and hustled after the server. He tapped her on the shoulder and, in simple and confident tones, asked that they change Brittany's order from steak to salmon. The server corrected the order and then breezed back into the kitchen as Brad returned to his table. His cheeks were red with a mix of embarrassment and pride.

Perhaps this was just the kind of man he was. Completely selfless. Willing to go out of his way to correct a dinner order at a restaurant.

What a contrast to Conner Radley.

Dinner continued on without many hiccups. Brittany felt slowly at ease with Evan Snow beside her, even though all of his stories made her roll her eyes into the back of her head. Brad caught her eye during one particularly long story, and Brittany nearly burst into giggles. It was like Brad could read her mind.

As Brittany finished up her second glass of wine, friends of Heather and Nicole spontaneously entered the restaurant and occupied that half of the table with bubbling conversation. Brad received a phone call that took him to the neighboring hallway. This left Brittany and Evan in a sort of empty bubble.

And, armed with a healthy dose of alcohol, Brittany turned to Evan, looked him directly in the eye, and asked:

"So. Have you seen or heard anything from Conner these days?"

The corners of Evan Snow's smile fell toward the ground. The normally whip-smart and savvy businessman seemed to stumble at the question. He took another sip of his vodka cocktail, cleared his throat, and replied, "I guess I'm just about the same as everyone else. Haven't seen him at all since you asked for a divorce."

"And you have no idea where he might be?"

"No, I don't," Evan told her.

What was that flicker behind his eyes? Brittany leaned back in her chair, crossing her arms over her chest. Evan turned his eyes toward the far end of the restaurant, staring.

"If you'll excuse me. I just remembered I need to have a chat with the chef."

"I'm sure you do," Brittany returned, watching as he stood, corrected his suit over his shoulders, and breezed back toward the silver kitchen door.

As he walked, Nicole and Heather burst into laughter about something their newly-arrived friends had said. The laughter was a strange soundtrack to the chaos of Brittany's thoughts. She felt at a great distance from all of them.

Suddenly, Brad arrived back at the table, sliding his phone into his back pocket. His smile was endearing, the only bright light Brittany currently knew.

"Hey, I think I'm going to head out soon," Brittany said to him spontaneously. "Is there any way you could drive me home?"

Chapter Thirteen

When Brad had driven out to Evan Snow's restaurant to dine with Brittany and her cousins, he'd followed after Heather in her vehicle, alone in his. Now, outside in the sharp chill of the April evening, he watched as Brittany stepped lightly around his cop car, easing alongside of it, awaiting for the doors to unlock. The smile she flashed him from the other side of the car made his heart skip three beats.

"Can I be your deputy, sheriff?" she teased as she entered the car, snapping herself beneath the seatbelt. She'd brought a gorgeous wave of perfume, a smell that Brad's coffee-reeking cop car truly needed.

"You'll have to pass a series of tests first," Brad told her as he turned on the engine.

"What sorts of tests?"

"Um." Brad wracked his brain for a funny remark. *Was there a book somewhere he could buy on flirtation?* He felt woefully out of practice.

"We'll start with a car chase test," he said finally.

"All right. I think I can pass this one with flying colors. I never let the bad guy get away, well, except for what just happened at the warehouse, of course."

"I think you'll do just fine," Brad affirmed as he eased out from the parking lot behind the restaurant. "You have to be able to ease through bad traffic. You have to be able to drive over one hundred miles per hour at a moment's notice. And what's more? You have to do all of that with a donut in your hand."

Brittany couldn't contain her laughter. Once she caught her breath, she replied, "I had no idea that you guys did all your car chases with a donut in your hand."

"It's never talked about. But we need it for fuel," he told her.

She flashed him a sideway grin. "Impressive."

They drove the rest of the way to Brittany's place in comfortable silence. As he parked out front, Brittany informed him that her daughter, Valerie, planned to spend the night with a friend that night.

"It's her spring break. I feel like such a bad mother, not taking her somewhere special for her senior spring break. Like Florida. Or California. Or France."

"I guess you've had other stuff on your plate," he told her.

"Yeah, well." Brittany lifted her shoulder as her eyes glistened. "I'm sorry that I wanted to leave so early. I just— I don't always know how I feel about Evan Snow."

"I've heard a lot of people say that since I moved to Bar Harbor. But your cousin Nicole is dating him, so that has to count for something."

Brittany buzzed her lips. Her eyes lifted toward the moon that ballooned through the night sky overhead. "Do you want to come inside for one more drink?"

Brad's brain literally twitched with disbelief. "I can only have one," he told her.

"I'll hold you to it."

Back inside, Brad and Brittany marched past the table heavy with antique documents and files. Brittany waved a hand toward the table and muttered, "Ugh. That's tomorrow's problem." She then sauntered toward the kitchen, where she opened the fridge and drew out a bottle of Pinot Grigio and a beer for Brad.

"I imagine you're not a big wine drinker."

"Not really, no."

Brittany snapped the top off the Pilsner and passed it to him. She then poured her pinot into a glass and swirled it, watching the soft liquid take its course around and around.

"To answer your question," Brittany said, mostly to her wine glass, "Nicole hasn't confirmed or denied her relationship with Evan Snow. I know the Harvey Sisters say that he's the reason the Keating Inn is still open to this day. But I do know that he was friends with my husband. And I don't trust my husband or anyone he ever associated with. That's just how I feel."

Brad leaned against the opposite counter, where he faced her and crossed one ankle over the other. "Maybe we should interview him."

"I don't know. It's not like Evan Snow needs my money. He's got enough of his own," Brittany stated. "Maybe my senses are off. It's been a trying few days. By Friday, I might be blaming the postman for the robbery."

"I don't think anyone should distrust their instincts," he told her.

"Have you ever arrested someone based on instinct alone?" Brittany asked in disbelief.

"Kind of. But I've only ever really worked in sleepy towns where gossip is the main lifeblood. You hear something from someone and build an idea of what might have happened from there, usually," Brad told her.

"But still no gossip about who might have robbed me."

"Unfortunately, not."

Brittany lifted a shoulder toward her ear, tipped her glass between her lips, and then eyed him in a way that made Brad feel half-naked.

"Look at me. Blabbering on and on. You seem to know everything about me at this point. But all I know is... I ran into you last autumn at an auction, where you worked for your sister. And you were terribly kind. Your kindness continues. Will it ever run out?"

"I don't really think of it as kindness."

"Just tell me something about yourself, Officer Brad Wethers," Brittany tried. "Something that differentiates you from all the other donut-eating car-chasing cops out there."

Brad turned his eyes toward the ground as a shiver raced up and down his spine. There was no mistaking it now. This woman was flirting with him. Even if he'd just crawled out of a cave after twenty years without human contact, he would have picked up on that.

Plus, she'd invited him into her home.

"Um. Well. I got to Bar Harbor about three years ago," he told her.

"Have you lived alone that whole time?"

"Yes," he told her. "But I um. I suffered a loss back in Bangor. My wife, Janine. She died. It was a freak stroke. She was only forty years old."

"Oh my God." Brittany placed her wine on the counter, making a clinking sound. "I don't know what to say."

"You don't have to say anything," Brad told her. "I know, just as well as you do, that words don't do much of anything in the face of that grief. I just keep going. Keep to myself. It's a fine life here in Bar Harbor. I'm glad I stumbled into it."

Brittany pressed her lips together, contemplative. "You're right. Words are never enough. It's just that we feel like we should say the right thing in certain circumstances."

"I know."

Brittany and Brad held the silence for a long time. Brittany's eyes curved toward the ground. Finally, she said, "Would you like to talk about her?"

Brad shook his head tenderly. "Only to say that she was a wonderful person. A beautiful musician. Incredibly clumsy. And actually... I miss her every single day."

Brittany nodded simply. She seemed to take his story with open arms, holding onto it, making it feel worthy and warm.

Finally, she said, "I'm so glad you had one another."

"Me too. Grateful for every minute with her."

Again, silence. Brad didn't regret bringing Janine up, exactly. It just wasn't clear where the conversation was meant to go from there. *Was he too anxious to stumble through the parameters of a date? Hadn't they just been flirting? He needed to get a grip already.*

"I hate that the only man I've ever loved was Conner Radley," Brittany blurted out suddenly. "I hate it with every fiber of my being."

"I don't think you can choose who you love," Brad tried.

"Maybe. I don't know. I've gone over it again and again in my head for decades now. Why did he choose me? Why did I choose him? Why did I allow this nightmare into my life?" Brittany flung a hand toward the counter and whipped out a Kleenex, which she dabbed on either side of her eye, collecting black makeup.

"Gosh. I'm sorry. You were just talking about your wonderful wife, and then I turned things over to my crazy ex-husband," she murmured between sniffles. "I'm so sorry. I'm not normally like that."

"No. We were both stewing in our separate despairs," Brad tried to joke. "Plus. This is a safe space. I think. Right?"

"Ever since Conner left, it is," Brittany said with another sniffle. She added then, "It just makes me question myself and whether I can trust myself at all, you know? Now that I'm out of that relationship, I'm hoping I'll become this whole other person who makes absolutely zero mistakes."

"I hate to break it to you," Brad interjected with a crooked smile.

"I know. I know." Brittany's laughter was alight with music. "I sound like the stupidest person on earth. But every day after he left, I've been on this quest to like myself more, you know. To remind myself that I deserve something more than what I've had."

What a contrast to his own life, Brad thought. Every day after Rachel's death, he'd watched himself as a bump on a log within his own life, performing his necessary tasks as police officer and returning home to sandwiches and bad television. What sort of life was that? Did he think that, with Janine's death, his own was over, too?

"You deserve so much more," Brad repeated Brittany's words, unsure of what to say.

"And you deserve to keep living," Brittany told him with a tilt of her head. "I think your wife would have wanted it that way."

"I know she would have," Brad whispered. "But I just don't know if I truly can."

Chapter Fourteen

That Saturday, the Harvey Sisters suggested another get-together to decompress after the difficult week. Brittany gave them a begrudging "yes," despite feeling that actually, she wanted to stay in the shadows of her home and hide from the world.

"I don't think they really understand what it means to have your entire livelihood taken out from under you without any answer," Brittany complained to Valerie, throwing her arm into a bag of chips and coming up with crunchy, salty slabs.

Valerie, an introvert through and through and therefore accustomed to this instinct to stay home, insisted this wasn't the right way to live. "This is a dark time, Mom, but we can make the best of it. Besides, Nicole always cooks the best meals."

It was an unusual thing for Valerie to drive them, as their mother-daughter relationship wasn't used to the role reversal. Brittany enjoyed it, stretching her legs out in front of her and operating the Bluetooth, playing songs from the nineties and bobbing her head along with the beat. Valerie told her mother she was "so lame" but said it in a way that exuded love and silliness. For a brief moment on the drive, Brittany was able to convince herself all the trauma of the past six months didn't belong to her.

En route, they stopped at the grocery store to buy fancy cheeses, bottles of wine, and plenty of juicy strawberries, raspberries, and blueberries, which Brittany ate distractedly as they eased the rest of the way to the Keating House. As Valerie parked out front, Brittany eyed the old inn, where she'd spent approximately four thousand hours of her life as a youngster.

"When I see the place, I can still smell the old cleaner we used to use," Brittany said under her breath. "It's like a nightmare that will never leave me alone."

Valerie laughed good-naturedly as she removed the keys from the ignition and flashed them across her lap. After another pause, she whispered, "I think about Grandpa all the time. About where he is. About whether he can see us."

Brittany shifted her eyes toward her daughter, surprised at the dream-like words she'd gifted her.

"I know he can feel the love we still have for him," Brittany told her softly before adding, "but I have to hope he didn't hear what I just said about the cleaning supplies. He was too good to me, and I never wanted anything to do with the business he built from the ground up."

Valerie gave her mother a sneaky smile.

"What? Is that smile meant to tell me that you don't want anything to do with Bar Harbor Antiques?" Brittany teased. "Because if it is, you don't have to worry yourself about that. I'm happy for you and Thomas to do whatever you want. I've always said that, and I've always meant it."

"If only it was so simple to know what you wanted to do..." Valerie said simply. "I know that you've always known. What a blessing that must have been."

Just then, Luke's big white truck creaked into the driveway beside them. He waved a sturdy hand, pulling them from their reverie. Valerie and Brittany stepped out into the spitting rain and hustled after Luke toward the comfort of the front porch.

"How's your Saturday going?" Luke asked as he opened the knob, delivering that sterling, handsome smile of his.

"Not bad. Who's operating the Acadia Eatery while you and Nicole are both here?"

"I'm just here for an hour or two, and then I'll head over to man the Saturday night crew," Luke told them. "I have my preppers over there slicing and dicing vegetables as we speak."

"Lucky them..." Brittany said sarcastically.

With the door open, spiced warm air swirled out from the Keating House kitchen, where Nicole whipped up a roasted duck as music from the sixties spit out from the speakers. Heather and her daughters, Kristine and Bella, stood around the kitchen table, sampling a new selection of natural wines from a local realtor. Recently. Valerie had really taken to both Kristine and Bella and greeted them warmly, rushing them for big hugs. Brittany knew that Valerie honored the girls' lives in New York City; she probably thought of them as the sleekest, the most fashionable, the most in-the-know. Brittany wished she could tell her daughter that nobody in the world— not Rihanna or Julia Aniston or Prince William— knew what they were doing. She wanted to tell her that everyone was making everything up all the time.

But that was something you had to learn for yourself.

"How's it going, cuz?" Heather wrapped Brittany in a hug as Kristine and Bella gabbed to Valerie about some purse they'd recently purchased in Brooklyn.

"Oh, fine. Well, if I'm honest, Valerie dragged me out today. I wanted to cower in sadness in my house."

"It makes sense," Nicole said, her spoon whipping around a big scoop of mashed potatoes. "I spent like a whole year wallowing at Casey's house after my divorce."

"You didn't wallow." Casey stepped into the kitchen in a

big red sweatshirt and a pair of jeans. There was a pen mark on her cheek, which Heather pointed out almost immediately.

"Gosh. I've been editing the blueprints all morning and making notes. I guess I got carried away," Casey admitted.

"It's usually better if you use the paper instead of your face," Heather teased.

"Anyway," Casey continued. "Nicole, you didn't wallow. You were with a manipulative man for many years. Brittany, you too. The fact that both of you have the strength to push yourselves beyond those relationships means you're some of the strongest women I know. Pat yourselves on the back."

"Okay. Now you sound like a kindergarten teacher," Nicole teased, rolling her eyes.

"No. It's nice," Brittany began. "Really. Thank you. I probably can't hear that enough."

"Tell us what happened with you and Brad after you left the restaurant the other night." Heather gave Brittany a mischievous glance.

"Mom?" Valerie, who seemed to have the ears of a dog, stepped out from her conversation with Kristine and Bella to ask, "What is she talking about? That officer?"

"Oh gosh, honey, it was nothing," Brittany returned quickly.

Behind her, Nicole reprimanded Heather for bringing up the "thing with Brad."

Hurriedly, Brittany talked over them, assuring her daughter that Brad was nothing but a friend. "He stopped by to tell me where he's at with the case."

"Why didn't you tell me?" Valerie demanded.

"Because he hasn't found out much yet, to be honest," Brittany offered. "But he's on it. He's working tirelessly." She then gave Heather a sharp glance, one that told her just how little she appreciated that "opening of a can of worms."

The Harvey-Keating family sat down for roasted duck at

two that afternoon. Heather poured them out beautiful glasses of natural wine, which Brittany had never had but soon learned was "all the rage in Brooklyn." Heather discussed the fact that her book's movie adaptation would soon begin filming, while Casey talked about the recent breaking-ground of the Keating House Part Two.

"It's been such a mess," Casey announced. "I've worked with many different weather patterns and many different construction teams. The guys I hired here seem incompetent. And on top of that, the construction workers complain that it's a little chilly when it's under forty degrees. Guys, welcome to Maine."

Mid-way through dinner, Nicole's daughter, Abby, arrived back from her shift at the Keating Inn, where she worked the front desk. She greeted Kristine, Bella, and Valerie warmly and then loaded her plate up with a feast.

"It was a wild ride today at the inn," she told them as she shoveled her food from her plate to her mouth. "A woman was screaming at a man who everyone thought was her husband. But in the center of the lobby, she told him to just go back to his wife already. She was like, '*It's over, Billy!*'"

"Oh my God," Heather cried, drawing a hand across her mouth. "I love the drama at that place."

"That's nothing," Brittany countered. "The things I used to see there back in the nineties are fodder for any soap opera. Every day, a new affair. One time, a guy threatened to throw himself out the window, and one of the maids who worked there at the time had to talk him down. Once, a young couple of around eighteen or nineteen came in and pretended to have forgotten their wallets. My father was a softie, especially back then, and he still let them have a room. They ended up staying for nearly a month. My father didn't question it, that is, until they tried to sneak out without paying the bill. It turns out they were on the run from the law. They'd robbed a bank down in

Nashville and driven all the way there. It was so romantic to them."

"What happened to them?" Kristine asked, captivated.

"I guess they were taken back to Nashville and tried for their crimes," Brittany offered.

"Look it up!" Bella cried.

Brittany groaned, grabbed her phone, and began to attempt to type in words that would give her the results she so desired. "Nashville Bank Robbery," however, gave her too many searches, and by the time she tried out, "Nashville teenage couple bank robbery," the conversation at the table had moved forward without her.

As Brittany slipped her phone back into her pocket, she received a sudden alert from Candace, a woman in charge of a nearby antique auction happening later that afternoon.

CANDACE BERGMAN:

Hello, Brittany. I received all that information about your stolen items. It broke my heart, but I never imagined I might encounter one of your pieces at this very show.

I believe one of the French wardrobes you listed might be here.

It's unclear if the person selling it has any idea of its true origin (if it's yours). Maybe you know her— a little old lady in the antique community. Nobody you'd ever suspect.

In any case, I feel that you should come here as quickly as you can to see the piece and confirm it's yours.

We have to look out for each other in the antique community.

Love to you and hope that you retrieve all the things you once lost.

Brittany's eyes widened with surprise. As she quickly reread the message, she nearly dropped her phone to the ground.

"Mom. What's going on?" Valerie demanded, her voice cutting through the hubbub of the surrounding conversation.

Brittany made heavy eye contact with her daughter. "I just got word that one of the pieces might be at an auction."

"What!" Heather cried.

"You're kidding." Nicole's jaw gaped open.

"No." Brittany passed her phone to Nicole, who read the message, her eyes widening.

"You have to call Brad," Heather instructed simply.

"I'm not sending him in my place," Brittany affirmed.

"No, but maybe he could go with you," Nicole suggested.

"I'm going, too," Valerie insisted.

"You guys stay here. Enjoy the food," Brittany told them as she stood up, grabbing her phone to search out Brad's number. Her thoughts whirred at a million miles a minute. Was it really possible that she could track down one of her pieces later that afternoon? What if it wasn't her piece? Would the sorrow of that destroy her?

"I'll pack you guys some snacks," Nicole said, leaping to her feet.

Brad answered the phone after only two rings, perhaps proof that he did very little on weekends. Or, it was proof that he would have answered a call from Brittany no matter where he was or what he was doing. It was difficult to say.

"Brittany. Hi, how is your weekend?"

"Brad. I just got word that one of the antiques might be nearby at an auction."

Instead of sounding shocked, Brad said, instead, a simple, "Okay, I'll drive. Where are you? I'll pick you up in ten minutes."

He was the sort of man she could count on, ready to go at a moment's notice. Brittany couldn't have asked for anything better.

Chapter Fifteen

Valerie sat timidly in the back of Brad's police car with one leg crossed gingerly over the other. Brittany gave her a soft yet unsure smile as she buckled herself in up front. "You comfy back there?" Brittany asked.

"Yeah. I could get used to this view," Valerie teased.

"Uh oh. Have I got another criminal on my hands?" Brad eased into the driver's seat in ordinary clothing: a pair of jeans, a dark green button-down shirt, and a pair of leather shoes, which didn't seem like anything Brad could have possibly picked out himself.

Perhaps that had been the work of the wife, Brittany thought. Perhaps she'd had a flair for fashion. Perhaps she'd left Brad with enough "gear" to get started in the dating world after her absence, only for him to live out multiple years in solitude, mourning her.

"You got a route for me?" Brad asked as he started the engine.

"It's about an hour and a half away," Brittany told him as

the map flashed up on the screen of her smartphone. "We're going to get on the highway and head west."

Brad gave her a firm nod, proof that he was prepared for the mission ahead. Brittany's heart leaped into her throat. Was this really happening? Suddenly, her phone dinged with a message from the auction organizer, Candace.

"Candace just sent me a photograph of the wardrobe. I'm about ninety-nine percent sure it's my piece."

"You don't say..." Brad muttered, incredulous.

"Let me see," Valerie instructed.

Brittany passed her phone back to Valerie, who inspected the eighteenth-century French wardrobe, her eyebrows pressed low.

"The detail over the handles..." Valerie muttered.

"I thought the same thing. The detail of the one we bought was too precise, too unique. It has to be that one," Brittany affirmed as she took her phone back.

"And did she say who's selling it?" Brad asked as he pressed his foot deeper on the gas pedal, whipping them toward the highway.

"Let me text her. I'm sure she's so busy..."

"Who would be so stupid as to take the piece only an hour and a half away and sell it within the same auction circles you normally operate in?" Brad demanded.

"That's a good question," Valerie affirmed. "Maybe they thought they could filter out the sales here and there. Never too many items at once... And get the revenue that way?"

"If they thought that, they severely underestimated Brittany Keating," Brad affirmed.

Brittany's lips parted in surprise. Her eyes turned to gaze at him, this strong man with this perfect profile, a dominant nose and the beginnings of a five o'clock-shadow that made him all the more handsome, and marveled at the sincerity of his words.

He truly respected her. He respected her in ways that it had never occurred to Conner Radley to respect her.

As luck would have it, that Saturday afternoon, a local radio station was having a Beatles marathon— highlighting everything from *Sergeant Pepper's Lonely Hearts Club Band* to *Please, Please Me* and everything in between. Brad turned out to be something of a Beatles know-it-all, usually calling out the album, the title name, or the year of release before the radio DJ did.

"Oh. This is my favorite one," he called as he turned the volume dial. "'Golden Slumbers.' Gosh, it's gorgeous, isn't it? I know Paul's kind of a nerd, that it's cooler to like John or George better. But Paul's cheesiness just speaks to me, you know?"

"Are you saying you'd describe yourself as cheesy?" Valerie teased from the back.

"That's right, Valerie. I'm taking ownership over my cheesiness," Brad told her proudly, just as the chorus for "Golden Slumbers" roared through the speakers. "Listen to that emotion! If feeling things is lame, then I don't want to be cool."

Valerie and Brittany erupted with laughter, both genuinely surprised that they could find such joy during such a dark time. But there was also an adventurous spirit to that afternoon, as though they were fighting for their lives, for their livelihood, which was represented with this beautiful eighteenth-century antique.

When they arrived at the auction house, Brad parked the cop car a bit away from the rest of the parking lot. Brittany took deep, ravenous breaths as she exited the vehicle, terrified, suddenly, of what would happen next. Brad retrieved Valerie from the back of the car, apologizing that you couldn't open the door from the inside.

"You'd probably have a whole lot of trouble on your hands if the back door of a cop car could open," Valerie joked.

They walked in silence toward the double-wide doors of the warehouse. Midway through the parking lot, the muffled roar of the auctioneer's voice reached their ears. The familiarity of it lifted Brittany's spirits. At the age of sixteen, at an auction for the Keating Inn, she'd fallen head-over-heels with antique auctions, a space that required instincts and quick action. It was there in the chaos that Brittany was allowed to forget herself. It was there that she truly shined.

Brad, Brittany, and Valerie stepped through the double-wide doors and into the throng of auction-goers, who hovered around the seated bidders, watching the action. Just then, a lamp from the forties was reaching the mid-two-hundreds, with several hungry buyers still bidding.

"I wouldn't give two dollars for that lamp," Brittany whispered into Valerie's ear, making her daughter shiver with laughter.

"What did you say?" Brad hissed, his eyes alight.

It was adorable that he wanted in on the joke. Brittany began to explain— that the lamp was a clear knock-off of a much bigger designer at the time, but at that moment, Candace bustled toward them, her eyes shining with the weight of her anxiety.

"There you are!" Candace cried, throwing her arms around Brittany.

Candace was something of a mother hen in the antique community. She weighed maybe ninety-five pounds, was nothing but bones and muscle and hard-earned antique knowledge. She'd once owned one of the most prominent antique collections in New England but had recently sold all of it, purchased a gorgeous home from the eighteen-hundreds, begun dating a man ten years her junior, and busied herself only with auction organization, which she adored.

"I was just so worried about you," Candace hissed as she gathered Brittany's hand in hers.

"Oh, Candace. Thank you for saying that. It's been a really trying time."

"The piece is still in the back. I haven't told Fran that we won't put it up for bidding."

"Fran? Fran Lyle?" Brittany's heart lifted with surprise. Fran Lyle had been in the antique business just as long as Candace and had similar "mother hen" energy. When Brittany had first met her, Fran had outbid Brittany on a beautiful ochre-colored couch from the fifties, which Brittany still dreamt about. It was then that she'd learned Fran's sense of style was top-rate.

"I tried to ask her about the piece," Candace breathed. "Without giving too much away."

"What did you ask?"

"Where she got it," Candace explained. "Who'd sold it to her in the first place."

"And what did she say?"

They breezed into the dark shadows of the back of the warehouse, which had been separated from the auction itself. Back there, the auctioneer's voice was muffled and inarticulate, just a strange whipping noise that echoed.

"She didn't know a lot about the person she'd gotten it from. It was an online sale, something her daughter had spotted and told her mother about," Candace explained.

"It makes sense. Fran doesn't seem like a regular internet user," Brittany said.

"Right. And maybe that made her the perfect target. She said the person didn't know much about antiques. Didn't know what he had on his hands."

"What did she pay for it?"

"Around a thousand."

"Wow. Yeah. That's a whole lot less than what we paid last weekend."

Who had stolen her antiques without understanding the value of what they took? Brittany's head spun with confusion.

They arrived before the eighteenth-century French wardrobe, which was positioned a bit away from the other antiques up for auction. It was as though it had entered Brittany's life via a dream.

"Yep. That's it. The last time I saw it was in Lake George," she whispered.

"I thought so..." Candace exhaled simply.

"But Fran doesn't have any paperwork to back up the sale?" Brittany demanded. "Nothing to indicate who this guy was?"

"Apparently, her daughter and son-in-law went to pick it up and forgot to bother with all that," Candace continued. "In any case, I'll explain the situation to Fran."

"But then, Fran's out a thousand dollars," Brittany pointed out.

"Fran knows better than this," Candace affirmed simply. "She should have gone with her daughter. She should have made sure of the paperwork. Maybe she's getting soft in her old age."

Brittany placed her hands tenderly on the gorgeous wood of the wardrobe and heaved a sigh. Her heart ached for all of them—for Candace, for Fran, and for herself. This was only one piece, one piece in a collection that had been meant to flesh out the entirety of the gorgeous building on South Main. *How could she possibly track all the other pieces down? Would it mean endless driving across New England, endless robbing of older women like Fran?*

She didn't like it one bit. But what choice did she have?

"Thank you again, Candace..." Brittany whispered.

"It's going to be a long road," Candace affirmed, as though she read Brittany's mind. "But you're a fighter. You always have been."

Brittany wanted to point out to her that actually, she'd been in an emotionally abusive marriage for over twenty years, which probably proved she wasn't much of a fighter at all. But she figured that was a moot point.

"I'll make the arrangements to have it shipped back to Bar Harbor," Brittany said. "Until then, though, can you hold it here at the warehouse for me?"

"Of course. That's just fine," Candace agreed. "I have to get back out front. I hope you'll stay a little while? Have a glass of wine or a snack at the break."

Brittany, Brad, and Valerie decided to stick around at least until the break, as it allowed them breathing room between long drives. They hovered in back, listening as the auctioneer rattled off the numbers.

"We'll start out at five hundred. Five hundred, do I see five hundred? Six hundred, I see six— no, seven hundred..."

"It's almost like music," Brad breathed into her ear.

"You're right," Brittany affirmed. "I've never thought about it like that."

At intermission, Brad, Brittany, and Valerie stood in line for drinks, eavesdropping on the surrounding antique dealers who bragged about what they'd picked up so far. A few of them greeted Brittany, although others seemed to avoid her like the plague, as though she represented bad luck in the industry.

Brittany scanned her surroundings as Brad ordered them a beer, a wine, and a soda for Valerie. Familiar faces abounded— but one caught her particularly off-guard. In fact, it took her eye a full five seconds to fully recognize who it was.

With a gasp, Brittany gripped Valerie's elbow.

"Val. Do you see who I'm seeing? There in the corner?" She whispered it as though the man far off in the distance could possibly hear her over the din of gossip.

"Who?"

Valerie followed Brittany's gaze across the sea of antique

dealers to finally, finally, latch on to the truly horrible sight in the distance.

There in the corner, surveying the crowd angrily, was Evan Snow.

And just as Brittany prepared to walk over to demand what the heck he was doing there, Evan's eyes connected with hers.

Just like a frightened rabbit, he slipped out of sight.

"I'm going after him!" Brittany cried, popping out of line just as Brad turned back with the drinks.

"What's going on?" he demanded of Valerie.

"Mom just saw Evan Snow," Valerie explained, just as Brittany dropped out of earshot.

As Brittany hunted for Evan, she wracked her mind for some rational reason why Evan might have been at the auction that day— the very auction where one of her stolen pieces had popped up.

Evan Snow had never demonstrated any desire for antiques, at least not to Brittany. Probably, his hotels, restaurants, and many homes had a series of beautifully designed pieces, but those had almost assuredly been picked out by someone else. Plus, the Harvey Sisters were having a party that would probably go late, and Evan Snow wasn't normally one to miss a Harvey Sister party.

Did he really have something to do with the stolen antique? Had he come there to see how much Fran got for it? Did he plan to steal that money from Fran somehow?

But again, Brittany returned to the same fact from before: Evan Snow had more money than God. What did he care about a few thousand dollars?

By the time she reached the far end of the warehouse, she spun back and made eye contact with Brad and Valerie, who shook their heads in disbelief. Clearly, Evan Snow had run out of there as quickly as he could. There was no catching him now.

Chapter Sixteen

"**M**om, you have to be careful."

Valerie sat with her arms crossed, glaring up at her mother from the back seat of Brad's cop car. Brittany seethed in the front seat, her eyes glued to the Keating House, which glowed with yellow warmth, the very portrait of a "before" photo, as though the universe already knew Brittany was about to storm inside and tell Nicole the truth about the person she'd fallen head over heels for. They'd already been in the driveway for a good three minutes, as Brittany wanted to consider what to do next. Perhaps obviously, she hadn't come up with a solution besides "storm in and curse Evan Snow once and for all."

"She has to know who she's involved with," Brittany muttered menacingly. "She didn't grow up here. She doesn't have the background history on the Snow family. How could she have known?"

"Okay, let's not jump the gun right now. All we know is this," Brad tried. "You spotted him at the auction where your wardrobe turned up a week after it was taken from you. That doesn't necessarily mean he was the culprit."

Brittany cast him a glance that was about as good as a word-less threat. Brad shrugged and added, "There's a whole lot of reasonable doubt. That's all I'm saying."

"Well, he still owes us an explanation," Brittany blurted, tossing her weight into the car door and darting toward the front porch, where she yanked open the door and rushed into the warm air of the foyer.

Inside the living room, the rest of the family was in the midst of a slightly-drunken round of charades. Entering it was like walking into a beautiful family sitcom, one where all the silly problems were wrapped up in a tidy bow by the end of the final scene.

Heather was in the midst of acting out her charade as Brit-tany gallivanted in. Tipsy, she flung her arms out to greet Brit-tany, crying, "She's back! Tell us everything! Did you catch your thief?"

One after another, Kristine, Bella, Nicole, Abby, and Casey turned back to eye Brittany curiously, several with salty snacks lifted to their lips. Brittany felt like the sideshow at a circus. She nearly crumbled to her knees with fatigue.

She wouldn't embarrass Nicole in front of her entire family. It was too much.

"Nicole, do you mind if I talk to you for a moment?"

Besides a simple twitch of her eyebrow, Nicole maintained a cool and calm demeanor, proof of her long hours as a chef. "Of course." She grabbed her glass of wine and stepped lightly around the couch, waving a hand toward Heather. "You can keep going, Heather. I don't think anyone's going to guess what it is with you doing that endless flailing of your arms technique, but you can keep trying if you want to."

Heather stuck out her tongue playfully, even as her eyes glittered with curiosity. "Do you girls have secrets to swap?"

"That's right," Nicole teased right back. "You're not invited."

Brittany closed both doors that led to the kitchen, latching her and Nicole in tight. The kitchen was thick with smells of roasted duck, baked brownies, buttered asparagus and spilled wine. It was intoxicating. Brittany grabbed a bottle of wine and poured herself a glass as, outside, she heard both Brad and Valerie enter the Keating House, greeting everyone with bright hellos.

"You're kind of freaking me out," Nicole finally admitted, leaning tenderly against the counter as Brittany chugged one-quarter of her glass in a single go.

"I'm freaking myself out, too," Brittany admitted. "But we've just had a whirlwind of an afternoon."

Silence filled the space between them. Brittany marveled that she'd only just met this woman a few years before— that their story was entirely too short and would remain so. Nicole adored Evan Snow. With Brittany's news, would Nicole retreat away from Brittany, targeting her unconsciously as the reason for her fledgling relationship's downfall?

"The wardrobe was my wardrobe," Brittany affirmed with a rasp. "Which was exciting and exhausting, all at once."

"That's fantastic news," Nicole offered. "You're having it shipped back?"

"Yes."

"Then what's the problem?"

Brittany swallowed the lump in her throat. Nicole's eyes widened as the tension between them grew.

"I might faint if you don't tell me soon."

"Evan was there," Brittany blurted. "Evan was in the corner of the auction, and when I tried to approach him to ask him why he was there, he fled. He literally ran away from me."

All the color drained from Nicole's cheeks. She looked like a deer in headlights. Complete shock swept across her face.

"What are you talking about? Why would Evan be at an antique auction?"

Brittany's nostrils flared. *Would Nicole actually tell her she didn't believe her? Would Nicole side with Evan over family?*

"I don't know. All I know is, when I asked him the other day if he's still in contact with Conner, he acted very strange," Brittany whispered. "It was like he knew something. And then he shows up at the place where my wardrobe was being sold off? Whatever it adds up to, it doesn't look good for Evan."

Nicole's hand tightened around the stem of her wine glass. After a pause, she drank it back, gulping down the rest, and placed the glass back on the counter with a terrible clank.

"Can Brad drive me?" Nicole demanded suddenly.

"Nicole... It doesn't have to be now."

"No, it does have to be now," Nicole told her pointedly, rushing toward the kitchen door to press it open. "I can't believe this. I can't believe I always do this."

"What do you always do?" Brittany asked, suddenly terrified of the monster she'd created.

Nicole snapped her eyes back to find Brittany's. "I always date the most horrendous of men. It's like a unique talent I have but don't want. I should be given an award."

Nicole darted down the hallway with Brittany hustling behind to keep up with her. When she reached the doorway to the living room, there was the picture of Nicole pointing a finger toward Brad, demanding, "You good to drive? We're headed to the Snow Estate."

Brad's eyes darted toward Brittany's. Valerie groaned and placed her head in her hands.

"What's going on?" Heather demanded. "Why are you going to Evan's right now?"

"It's a long story, Heather," Nicole replied flippantly. "I'll tell you another time."

"Wow, okay!" Heather cried as Nicole flashed toward the

coat rack, grabbing her coat and whipping it across her shoulders.

"Don't take it to heart," Valerie said hurriedly. "Mom just broke her world in two."

"We'll be here when you girls get back," Casey said, scowling with worry. "But then we'll need an update on everything. You understand?"

Not wanting Nicole to have to sit in the back by herself, Brittany piled in beside her and watched as Nicole's cheeks twitched violently, matching her whirling thoughts as they drove out to the Snow House. Brittany could see so many of her own thoughts about Conner echoed back in Nicole's expression.

Would they ever be able to trust anyone, ever again?

Was romance ever worth it?

Was the world out to get them?

Brittany had never actually been on the other side of the thick iron gate that wrapped around the Snow Property. When they reached it, they discovered, to her sincere surprise, that the gate was wide open. *Had Evan Snow let down his defenses? Did he think he was now indestructible?*

When they parked closer to the mansion itself, Nicole pushed herself against the door, attempting to get out. Brad and Brittany, both explained it didn't work like that, that you had to wait for it to be opened from the outside. But Nicole's anger made it difficult for her to understand.

Up at the front door, Brittany watched in awe as Nicole brought out her jangle of keys, one of which slipped easily in the keyhole. *Had Nicole and Evan's relationship reached such heights?* It was a big deal to get a key— a big deal to make that step. Brittany's stomach clenched with sorrow. *Were women like she and Nicole always doomed to make the same mistakes?*

The foyer of the elaborate Snow Mansion was shadowed, dark, with only the sinister carvings of various old-world statues peeking their heads out from far corners. Nicole stormed through the foyer, making her way down a hallway, daring both Brittany and Brad to catch up.

When they reached Evan's study, however, they found the desk gleaming with lack of use, all folders stacked and organized, and the laptop black.

"Where is he?" Nicole growled.

"We don't have to go through the whole place," Brittany tried, even as Nicole bucked back, darting down the hallway and toward Evan's top-of-the-line gym, where, apparently, he sculpted his body in front of an enormous television screen.

"His cars..." Nicole muttered, rushing again down the hallway and toward one of Evan's three garages, where he kept some of the ritziest vehicles in Bar Harbor: a Ferrari, a Lamborghini, a Mercedes Benz, and another vintage vehicle from the fifties, which he'd occasionally driven through Bar Harbor's yearly Fourth of July parade. Brittany had always thought this to be reckless. Bar Harbor detested the Snow Family. Who was to say they wouldn't destroy his vehicle, throw milkshakes in his face, or ridicule him in some other way?

Of course, this was Bar Harbor, a family-friendly society where it was expected you do the right thing, no matter what.

Nicole rushed through the door between the main house and the first of the garages with such severity that Brittany half-expected the door to swing off it's hinges. With the door wide open, they discovered that for one-half of this particular garage, a vehicle had been removed, and a wide, cavernous space allowed refuge for two beautiful, old-world antiques... an Italian-made sofa from the early twentieth century and the gorgeous desk that Valerie had hand-selected for the collection. The Chinese Chippendale.

Evan Snow stood alongside the antiques, his face surly, his arms crossed over his chest. His expression reflected back no sign of surprise. In fact, he seemed as though he waited for them to come.

"Evan." Nicole stopped dead between the doorway and the antiques, her voice wavering only slightly.

She'd learned a thing or two since her narcissistic husband had left her.

She'd gained some confidence that would serve her.

"Evan... I don't even know what to say to you. Except... How could you? How could you do this to my family? I trusted you. Even after so many people warned me about you— I trusted you."

"Nicole..." Evan tried his voice in warning.

"And to think of it. You're Evan Snow! We're literally standing directly next to your Lamborghini. And you decide to go out of your way to steal this woman's entire inventory of antiques, right when she's on the brink of redesigning her life!"

"Nicole..." Evan interjected.

"Don't you dare 'Nicole' me," Nicole snapped, raising a finger to wag in his face. "I can't believe I thought for a minute that we were actually headed somewhere! That we were going to have a future together! That we..."

"Nicole! Dammit. I didn't do this!" Evan finally erupted. He looked like a boiling pot of water, bubbling over the sides and spilling out across the stovetop.

Nicole snapped her lips shut, shocked at his volatility and his answer. Brittany and Brad hustled on either side of her as Evan's eyes scanned them.

"If you didn't do this, why did you run away from me at the auction today?" Brittany demanded.

For the first time, Evan Snow looked hesitant and frightened. Stuttering, he slipped his fingers through his dark hair and answered, "I went there on a hunch, okay? I was still trying to put the pieces together. And I wasn't sure what I'd seen yet. When I spotted you, I panicked and ran out."

"A likely story," Nicole spat.

"I swear." Evan cleared his throat and added, "I had a tracker on my brother Elijah's vehicle. And I followed that tracker to the auction."

Nicole's jaw dropped. "You're kidding."

"I'm not." Evan grabbed his phone, flipping through the apps to show the tracker's location, which remained there at the warehouse where Brittany had seen him earlier that afternoon. "But I didn't see Elijah anywhere. He must have tricked me somehow. I don't know. But when I got back home, I found these here."

Evan then pulled open the top drawer of the wardrobe as Brittany shrieked, "Be careful with that! It's older than your mansion!"

But before she could hurl another insult about Evan Snow and his money, Evan showed her what lurked inside the drawer.

There sat a big white piece of paper on which someone had drawn a huge smiley face.

"That doesn't prove anything," Nicole blurted. "Anyone could have drawn that."

"The paper looks new," Evan pointed out. "If it had been in this wardrobe for a number of years, it would have been yellowed."

"There could be another explanation," Nicole added.

"Listen. Believe me or don't believe me. All I know is, I tried to track down my brother, I couldn't find him, and came home to these antiques in the garage."

"But why did you start to track your brother in the first place?" Brittany demanded.

Evan's eyes dropped toward the ground. He seemed to struggle with his answer but soon articulated it, still unable to meet Brittany's gaze.

"I have a hunch he's hanging out with Conner again," he

said simply. "And you're right, you know. He's the only one who could have been involved in this. He's the only one who has it out for you. And my brother's always up for madness, whatever it is. He gets off on getting away with stuff. The thing he hasn't reckoned for, I guess, is that I'm not a full-blown member of the Snow family any longer. I've been shown a different way to live."

Evan finally lifted his gaze toward Nicole. His eyes echoed back adoration, even love.

"Why should we believe you?" Nicole asked, her voice wavering dangerously.

"Again, you don't have to," Evan told her simply. "But I want to help you if you're open to that."

Brittany turned to find Brad beside her with his hand wrapped tenderly around his chin as he contemplated the current scenario. Brittany surprised herself, touching his shoulder.

"What do you think, Officer?" she asked.

Brad shook his head. "I'm going to have to get a statement from you down at the station, as you've been found with stolen inventory."

"I understand," Evan told him.

"Other than that..." Brad heaved a sigh of disbelief. "If you have some idea of where to go from here, Mr. Snow, I'm all ears. I have a hunch that Brittany's ex-husband is trying to make her crazy, even from afar. And I won't stand for it."

"Neither will I," Evan affirmed.

Chapter Seventeen

The eighteenth-century-built French wardrobe from Saturday's auction arrived at Brittany's antique shop at two-thirty p.m. that Monday afternoon. Brittany and Gabe watched as the hired movers eased the gorgeous piece from the small-sized moving truck and placed it gently in the very center of the Bar Harbor Antiques foyer, as though that was as good a place to put it as any. Brittany didn't have the strength to tell them where to move it and nearly let their strong muscles depart for the day before Gabe interjected and said, "Actually, could you move it to that space by the window? That's where we've decided to put it for future sale."

Disgruntled, the movers lifted the wardrobe and hobbled toward the window, where they placed the wardrobe almost gently alongside a night-table built in Rome from the 1870s. Brittany pulled out several bills to tip them and watched them go, her heart thudding in her ears.

"Thank you," she told Gabe under her breath. "When they put it down without asking me where it was supposed to go, I almost screamed."

"I'm here for you, Brittany," Gabe told her gently, padding her upper arm. He then retreated behind the coffee counter, where he made the espresso machine roar. Methodically, he crafted two perfect iced coffee drinks laced heavily with caramel and extra sugar. It was a monstrous thing for the waist-line, and Brittany hadn't bothered with spin class that morning. Even still, the thick milkshake-like liquid coursed across her tongue. Maybe this was the only real joy she'd get.

"It really is a spectacular piece," Gabe said as he rounded back toward the French wardrobe, which stood proud and regal, already altering the air of the greater space.

Brittany joined him. Her hand was placed tenderly on the top of the wardrobe. After another sigh, she added, "I have two more pieces being delivered today."

Gabe's eyes widened. "You tracked them down?"

"Not quite." Brittany wasn't sure how much she wanted to reveal about the situation with Evan Snow. Was he somehow manipulating the story to make her look foolish? Would she really allow herself to trust a Snow? "But whoever robbed me is trying to troll me. They dropped two pieces off at a— um a friend. One had a picture of a smiley face on the inside."

"That's so creepy," Gabe muttered.

Brittany scanned the drawers before her, suddenly conscious that this wardrobe, too, could hold some sort of taunt, perhaps from Conner himself. Unwilling to wait around for the thing to explode on her (or something equally as traumatic yet metaphorical), Brittany began to pull open the drawers, hardly being careful enough with such a pristine object.

"What are you doing?" Gabe demanded.

"Maybe there's something like that in here. A clue..."

The third row on the left revealed something, all right. When Brittany pulled it open, she found a heavy black object, on which a bright red dot flashed.

"What is that?" Gabe's voice was high-pitched, frightened.

"I'm not totally sure." Brittany grabbed her phone and dialed Nicole's number, gripping the heavy device with a stiff grip. Nicole answered on the second ring, bringing with her a sea of chaotic voices from the inside of the kitchen at the Acadia Eatery.

"Brittany. What's wrong?"

"Hey, could you do me a favor? Could you ask Evan if the tracker he put on Elijah's vehicle is still located at the warehouse? Or if it's changed locations?"

"Um. Okay, I can do that."

Brittany allowed a minute to pass. In the background, there came a hiss from a skillet and then Luke's voice, barking orders at a kitchen prepare.

"Are you're okay, Brittany?" Nicole asked finally.

Brittany flared her nostrils. Since their break-in at the Snow Estate, she wasn't entirely sure how she felt. She felt like a boat without a captain, a swimmer without a shore.

"I'll be fine," Brittany told her. "Just trying to put the pieces of my life back together is all."

When they got off the phone, another driver entered Bar Harbor Antiques. The bell jangled as he explained that he had a delivery from Evan Snow, already paid in full. Brittany nodded and immediately instructed him on where the pieces needed to be positioned. Her stomach questioned whether or not she should feel guilty for Evan Snow paying for this delivery. A voice in the back of her mind yelled out a resounding "no way."

Nicole texted back as the new delivery workers settled the desk in the corner.

NICOLE: Actually, Evan says that the tracker is located at Bar Harbor Antiques...

NICOLE: Are you okay, Brittany????

Brittany glared at the red blinking device, which she'd positioned atop the wardrobe. Was this proof that Evan told the truth? Or was this another set-up?

BRITTANY: I found it. I just wanted to make sure it was the same one.

NICOLE: But no sign of Elijah or Conner?

BRITTANY: Not unless they're in one of the other drawers. I haven't checked all of them yet.

"I want to be grateful you know?" Brittany opened the little glass container on the counter of the coffee shop area, hand-selecting a brownie and tearing it into little pieces, eating each gooey bit gingerly. "Grateful that I have these three pieces back. But I can't help but think of the twenty-two pieces still out there— how I hand-selected them for this next part of my life. How I couldn't wait to see how people would react to them when I put them in the store."

Gabe moaned inwardly. He stepped toward one of his paintings, adjusting the angle of it lovingly. Brittany felt as though they stood in a haunted house, one they could no longer open up to the public. The ghosts had tainted everything.

As though the universe wanted to tease her even more, Brittany's phone dinged with a message from an antique dealer located in Brunswick.

Brittany, hello. I don't know if you remember me. My name is Mallory, and we met several years ago at an auction outside of Portland. I've recently learned of your plight and happened to glance at the fantastic array of pieces that those criminals stole from you.

And then I took stock of my own collection.

It seems that I purchased something recently from an online seller—an Italian sofa. Find the photo attached.

Brittany's eyes widened. There it was— another of her pieces.

I thought the sale to be very strange. A young woman sold it to me for a price far below market value. I hate to say that I fell for this trap, but I suppose I was at the mercy of my own greediness.

In any case, I'd like to have it shipped to you as soon as possible. Can you confirm your last name and shipping address?

"Wow. Another one?" Gabe shook his head as he re-read the email. "It's nice that she's going to send it over here as soon as possible."

"It is nice. It is." Brittany sounded hesitant. "But I can't help but think that this is all a part of Conner's grand scheme. He knows it's driving me absolutely bonkers to receive these messages from all over the state. Plus, he's been profiting off of the sale of these items without knowing what he can ask for! It's such Conner Radley behavior, thinking he's smarter than everyone yet falling short."

Gabe clucked his tongue. "You are at the mercy of the worst kind of sociopath. A stupid one."

Brittany laughed, even as her eyes filled with useless tears. Conner would love to know he was making her cry. He always seemed to gain power when she wept.

But the strangeness of the day (along with its tears) had only just begun.

A few minutes later, Brittany got another similar email. And two hours later, another. By the end of the afternoon, four different antique dealers had admitted that they held one of Brittany's original pieces and were more than willing to have them shipped back. Brittany wept with a mix of delight and sorrow. She detested that these poor people, good people, had been taken advantage of! How she detested that Conner had extended his evils out across the antique world, a world she adored with her whole heart.

Armed with this fresh bout of information, Brittany drove out to the Keating House to discuss things with Nicole, Heather, and Casey. She also texted Brad, who informed her he was on "temporary duty of a downtown broken-down traffic light" but would contact her shortly about the potential next steps.

Brittany had no idea where they went from here. Each email delivered a tiny bout of hope, but gave almost no clues as to where the remainder of the items actually were. Perhaps this was Conner's biggest con of all.

When Brittany reached the Keating House, she entered without knocking to find a silent house, echoing with spring-time light. Exhausted, she collapsed on the couch, curled up in a ball with the corners of an Afghan throw across her legs. When she awoke, hissed whispers vibrated out from the kitchen, proof that whoever was there wanted to keep things quiet for the sake of her sleep.

But after a moment of clearing her head, Brittany could make out the voices.

It was Evan and Nicole.

"You have to believe me, Nicole. I don't know how many more times I have to tell you that I would never do anything to hurt your family," Evan breathed. "I've been falling in love with you since the moment I met you. And that love has only grown more powerful with each passing day."

"Stop, Evan..." Nicole sniffled, clearly distraught. "I no longer know how to trust anyone. I'm not sure if I'm up for something like this."

"Are you saying you don't believe me?" Evan demanded, taking a small step as though she had stabbed him in the chest.

"I'm saying that I don't know if I physically or emotionally can believe you after everything I've been through," Nicole breathed.

"Nicole. Please. I'm telling you the truth. The last thing I want is to hurt you or cause an issue with our relationship."

There was a sudden creak from the bottom step of the staircase. Brittany pulled her head around to discover Heather, dressed in cozy pajamas and a thick pair of socks. She joined Brittany on the couch, cuddling close to her. Nicole's sobs in the kitchen became muffled as she finally allowed Evan to hold her. Brittany's stomach twisted with the longing to be understood half as well.

"I think he might be telling the truth," Heather whispered. "Evan Snow, I mean. I know it's a struggle for you to trust him. You're probably right to be hesitant. But..."

"No. I think I do trust him," Brittany returned. "I just don't know what to do with that trust. He's the closest thing between me, Conner, Elijah, and my stolen inventory."

Brittany continued to explain the messages she'd received from members of the antique community, showing Heather the emails and the apologies and the offers to have them delivered back as soon as possible. As Heather read them over, Evan and a tear-soaked Nicole came out of the kitchen, holding hands. It seemed they would no longer pretend they were anything less than boyfriend and girlfriend.

"Nicole. You have to look at these," Heather ordered, flashing Brittany's phone toward her.

Together, Nicole and Evan read the emails, their brows furrowed. Brittany shivered anxiously, clasping her hands over her lap.

"You think this has Conner and Elijah all over it?" Nicole asked, lifting her eyes toward Brittany.

"Yes, especially after I found the tracker this afternoon," Brittany returned.

"Where are all these places located?" Evan asked, circling his finger over the phone.

"You mean, where are the antique shops who reached out today?" Brittany asked. "I haven't looked up all their locations yet."

"Let's do that," Evan suggested, pulling out his own phone.

Brittany used her search function to investigate the addresses of the Brunswick-based antique dealer, followed by one in Scarborough, one in Biddeford, and another just north of Portland, in Falmouth. As Brittany recited the town names, Evan made little dots around the map of his own phone, which created a near-perfect circle around the city of Portland.

"Huh." Evan showed Brittany this evidence. "I don't think it's crazy to think the rest of your pieces are somewhere in Portland."

"Great," Brittany sighed. "One of the biggest cities in Maine. I'm sure they'll be easy to find."

"There has to be a way," Evan muttered, wracking his brain.

As the others studied the map and its maniacal red dots, Brittany dialed her divorce lawyer, Mary, for an added layer of security. She wanted to pin this guy down.

"Hi, Mary. Maybe this isn't something you can answer. But I'm curious. Where is Conner's divorce lawyer located? City wise, I mean."

"Oh, he's over in Portland," Mary confirmed evenly. "Why do you ask?"

"No reason. Thanks a bunch, Mary."

"Any time."

Chapter Eighteen

round five-thirty, Brad Wethers finally arrived at the Keating House to discover Brittany, Heather, Nicole, Casey, and Evan in the midst of cooking up a yummy Thai-inspired dinner with peanut sauce, chicken, vegetables, and rice. A nourishing yet slightly spiced smell swirled out from the opened windows; laughter erupted out toward the heavens, proof that companionship, love, and family were all truly needed— even in the face of cruelty and adversity. Even in the face of so much loss.

Brittany had said on the phone that they had quite a lot to tell him, which had nearly sliced him in two. He'd felt the weight of every passing moment as he stood at the traffic light, lifting the ridiculous stop sign over his head and guiding drivers through. "I'm a detective," he'd muttered to himself once or twice throughout, irritated that he couldn't use his real skills and operated, instead, as a human traffic light.

After Brad knocked on the door, Brittany pulled the door open with a brilliant smile and her lips tinged red from wine.

She made her way toward him, hugging him for a split-second, before guiding him into the Keating House.

"We've had quite a day," she explained as Brad removed his shoes in the foyer.

"Is that Officer Brad?" Nicole peeked out from the kitchen, waving a large wooden spoon in greeting.

"Welcome back, Officer Brad!" Casey called out, raising her wine glass toward him.

"Do you guys ever do anything but hang out, drink wine, and prepare delicious meals?" Brad teased as he entered the kitchen, immediately accepting a glass of wine from Evan Snow.

"You got a problem with our style of living?" Nicole teased.

"I can't say that I do," he said as he dropped his head back, allowing the density of the Italian wine to coat his tongue.

"It's really something, isn't it?" Brittany asked after he swallowed.

Brad, overwhelmed with the brightness of her eyes and the gleam of her hair, nodded, unsure of what he answered for. "It really is."

Brad steadied himself against the kitchen counter as Brittany clasped her fingers together.

"Evan figured out that Conner's probably somewhere in Portland," she affirmed.

Brad's heart thudded strangely at the mention of Conner's name. To Brad, he was something like a villain in a comic book.

"And I confirmed it with my lawyer," Brittany continued. "Conner's lawyer lives in Portland, as well. It makes sense that he went there. I think he always missed bigger cities after he left Boston. But he needed to be close enough to torment me."

"Ugh. This guy is the worst!" Casey cried, exasperated.

"And it stands to reason that if he's in communication with Elijah... There will be clues around Portland as to where they've hung out," Evan Snow said, drawing a spatula through a large pile of sizzling veggies.

"What kind of clues?" Brad asked.

"Well, how should I put this?" Evan knocked the side of the skillet with his spatula. "Elijah has certain demands when it comes to his lifestyle. He wouldn't be caught dead in something like a TGI Fridays, for example."

"Which is his loss," Heather interjected. "They have brilliant quesadillas."

"That being said," Evan continued with a laugh, "There are only a select number of upper-echelon bars in the Portland area."

"We're planning to just start spamming them with phone calls tonight," Brittany explained.

"I'll pretend to be Elijah, saying I lost my credit card somewhere. If the person answering the phone acts like we know each other... That's a clue that Elijah and, presumably, Conner have spent a good deal of time there. And because Elijah is a creature of habit, I see no reason why the two of them wouldn't frequent that joint, especially during this exciting week for them, at the height of their outrageous con against Brittany."

"I can't get it in my head as to why Elijah would want anything to do with this," Casey said, disgruntled.

"Elijah just likes a good time," Evan told her. "And he's never gotten into any real trouble before. Our father got him out of the DUIs. When he was caught stealing in college, he was put on a probation period of, like, two months, and then it was written off his record. Money has been his defense through all of it, the reason he hasn't fallen apart. And I have to say. I'm so damn sick of it."

"Yeah!" Brittany cried, lifting her glass of wine toward the ceiling triumphantly. "Let's get 'em!"

"But first, let's eat. Coat our stomachs with some nourishing food." Nicole suggested coaxingly, collecting several plates from the cabinet and lining the dining room table.

A few minutes later, Abby and Valerie both walked through the front door. Afterward, Brittany's son, Thomas, arrived, hungry from a long day of lobster fishing. Brad watched as Brittany placed a gentle kiss on her children's foreheads; his heart swam with affection for her, for the love she had for the children she'd created with that monster.

What a strange thing it was to grow up, to meet so many others with such density to their stories. What a strange thing it was to find that he liked it, the growing older thing. Yes, he'd wanted to do that with Rachel, spend that time into infinity side-by-side. But God had had other plans.

"Val said that some more of your pieces popped up today?" Thomas asked his mother as they sat around the dining room table, their forks and knives clinking, their chairs shrieking against the hardwood.

"That's right," Brittany affirmed. "The plan is to get them all back!"

Thomas laughed outright, drawing a slab of chicken doused in peanut sauce to his lips. Brad wondered if Thomas knew that his father was their number-one suspect in his mother's robbery. How could a young man handle another huge blow to their already broken family dynamic?

As they ate, the conversation circled other avenues, other stories. Thomas talked about nearly falling into the Atlantic earlier that morning when a wave had snuck up on the lobster fishing boat and nearly cast him in.

"It scares me, you being out there on the water all the time," Brittany admitted.

Thomas chewed somberly; his eyes shadowed. "Then I guess maybe this is the right time to tell you that I was accepted into the University of Maine this morning."

Brittany threw her hands up on either side of her, dropping

her fork with a clank. "Thomas! You didn't even tell me you were applying."

She scrambled around the table as others in the Harvey-Keating clan roared with excitement. Brittany held her son tightly against her, her eyes closed. "I'm so proud of you," she whispered. "Really. I was proud of you before, but this... This is the next step toward your future. I really believe that."

Later, while Nicole, Casey, and Brittany cleaned up dinner, scraping plates clean and soaking the skillet, Thomas said goodbye to everyone, telling them he wanted to go celebrate his acceptance with some pals at a bar nearby. Brittany wished him well, waving a hand as he stepped out. When he left, her eyes remained on the closed door, as though she half-expected him to burst back through.

"He doesn't know about his dad, does he?" Nicole asked suddenly, demanding the same question that had been on Brad's mind.

Brittany blew air out between her lips. "Of all of us, Thomas had a pretty good relationship with Conner. They haven't spoken since Conner left, that I know of, at least. And his wanting to go to college is proof that he wants to extend himself beyond his father's career in the fishing industry. But still, I imagine it'll be a hard blow when we eventually have to tell him the truth."

"We have to catch him first," Evan affirmed, tapping his cell phone with the edge of his fingernail. "I think it's about time I make those calls."

Together, they gathered around the mid-century couch in the living room and watched as Evan dialed The Motley Crew, a swanky place on the top floor of a Portland high-rise that sold twenty-five-dollar cocktails and fifty-dollar appetizers. This suited the likes of Elijah Snow, apparently, even as it would have bankrupted Brad Wethers.

"Hi, there. It's Evan. Evan Snow." He spoke with unlimited confidence. Brad almost believed him, despite knowing the con. "I was curious if I left my credit card on file with you." Evan's cheek twitched as he listened to the response. It was clearly a disappointment. "Thank you anyway."

He hung up and shrugged simply. "They denied seeing my credit card, and they didn't know him. They pretended to, but there was no camaraderie."

"What do you mean?" Heather asked.

"I mean, Elijah is incredibly talkative. Wherever he goes, he makes friends with waiters and bartenders and busboys. If Elijah went there frequently, they would have greeted me much differently."

Evan continued to dial, one fancy top-dollar place after another. One place almost had Evan fooled until they asked him how to spell his last name.

"Are you kidding?" Evan demanded before hanging up. "They obviously weren't it."

After nearly an hour of this, Brad was on the verge of suggesting they give up for the night. Desperation lurked on each of their faces.

"Have you heard of this speakeasy?" This was Abby, curled up in a ball on the floor, leaning against the couch. She peered down at her phone, which seemed to reveal endless secrets.

"What speakeasy? It wasn't on my list." Evan replied.

"It's called The Minty Green," Abby recited. "It's not very well known on the scene yet. It seems like the place you'd go if you wanted to feel important and you had enough money to throw around."

Evan's eyes sparkled. "That sounds like Elijah's place. You got a number for me?"

Abby recited the phone number as Evan typed it in. Everyone waited with bated breath, both fearful this was another dead end and terrified that it wasn't.

"Hi, there. It's Elijah. Elijah Snow. And I—" Evan stopped

speaking as his lips curved toward his ears. He didn't even have to say the rest of what he'd prepared. It was clear—whoever was on the other end had already recognized his name.

"That's right. I was just calling to ask a question about the card I had on file at your establishment," Evan continued. "But I just found it in my things just now. Yeah. What? The Friday-night party? I already told you I wouldn't miss that for anything. I'll see you then, buddy. Thanks a lot."

Evan hung up the phone and turned his eyes to find Nicole's. They shared an intimate moment between them, captivated and excited by what Evan had finally managed to do.

"Apparently, there's a big jazz party Friday night," Evan said mischievously. "And Elijah has already told them he's coming."

"How can we be sure he'll be there?" Brad asked, crossing his arms tightly over his chest.

"We can't be sure," Evan returned with a shrug. "But it's the best plan we have so far."

"So, what are we going to do? Storm in and demand that he and Conner tell the truth?" Casey asked, incredulous.

They shared a moment of silence. It seemed that every step forward in their scheme revealed more holes in the plot. It was true that they needed some kind of confession. But as they didn't have any concrete evidence, Brad couldn't exactly storm in and arrest them.

"We need someone to go in and talk to them," Heather offered.

"Conner knows almost all of us," Brittany replied, her nails scratching the edge of her hairline.

Again, silence. Heather scrunched her nose tight, distracted. And a moment later, in the midst of the horrible density of confusion, Luke burst through the front door with a bright, "Hello! Is there any food left over? I smelled it from the driveway."

Heather's eyes widened with surprise. She leaped up, her hands widening as she said, "Luke! Your sister! Luke! Your sister!"

"Um. What about my sister?" Luke asked, his smile faltering as he removed his coat.

"A night of jazz! She plays the piano! She's literally a jazz musician!" Heather cried.

Luke shook his head with a mix of annoyance, confusion, and unquestioned love for the woman before him. "I never have any idea what you're talking about!"

"I think I have a hunch." Evan Snow began, his smile crooked. "And to be honest with you, Heather, it's genius. It really is."

Chapter Nineteen

"I don't know. I really don't know if I'm up for it." Angie said the words mostly to her coffee cup, her shoulders curved toward the ground. Behind her, an upright piano featured a number of framed photographs, including one of her daughter, Hannah that was taken recently in the Bar Harbor port. "I'm not what they'd call an ingenue," she continued. "I've never lied to anyone in my life, that I can remember. And even that was probably some kind of accident."

"None of us would purposefully lie," Brittany interjected. "But we don't know any other way to corner my ex-husband and prove his lies."

Angie placed her teeth against the curve of her lower lip and cast her gaze toward the floor.

Across from her, Brittany, Luke, and Heather sat expectantly, all sending prayers to heaven that she would agree to such a task. It was like living out the plot of a James Bond film. It was also risky and reckless. Brittany couldn't imagine what she'd have thought had she been in Angie's shoes.

"I don't even know if I have anything appropriate to wear to a place like this." Angie began, but with hesitation.

Luke smacked his hands together excitedly. "That's what Heather's for. You have something she can borrow, don't you?"

Heather blinked her ocean-blue eyes, allowing a thick moment to pass. "It's not that I wouldn't. It's just that I think you deserve your own things. Especially because you'll be doing this enormous task for us."

"No. That's so silly and such a waste." Angie countered.

"Wasteful? You're a musician. You need beautiful clothing to perform in," Heather affirmed. "Please, let us treat you."

Angie's face twitched with a mixture of regret and panic. Compared to the Harvey-Keating family, Angie had very little in the way of funds. The apartment was sparsely decorated and still rather somber— a place Angie called their "in-between" place before they picked up the pieces of their life and figured out how to flourish in Bar Harbor. In the corner, they'd collected a number of baby items, including a crib, a pile of adorable infant clothes, and little plush toys. Brittany knew it wasn't feasible for the two of them to remain in that apartment after the baby was born. Perhaps she and the rest of the Harvey clan could help out, put them up somewhere with a little more space, a little more sleeping room. The walls were incredibly thin and the air took in almost no sunlight.

But Brittany didn't know what it was like to have so little. Guaranteed, Angie was too proud to accept something like that. She was the sort of woman who wanted to work for it and Brittany had to respect that.

"Okay. Okay, okay," Angie blurted out, clasping her hands together as though she had already regretted it. "I'm not doing it just for the clothes, though. I've read about The Minty Green's jazz nights. This could be really good for my career."

"Yes!" Luke cried, jumping to his feet to give his newfound sister a big hug. "I'm so thrilled."

146

"But how the heck will you get me in?" Angie asked, her eyes widening as Luke wrapped his arms around her.

"Let's let Evan figure that out," Heather offered thoughtfully.

"Gosh. Me, a spy. I can't even picture it." Angie's laughter twinkled like music. She then turned her eyes toward her piano as a blush crept up her cheeks. "I'll have to put together a really fantastic set. Something that will make Elijah and this Conner guy want to talk to me."

"The way you play? The entire bar will want to talk to you," Luke told her.

"You're such a sap, Bro," Angie teased.

* * *

With Elijah Snow's clear connections at The Minty Green, it wasn't a difficult thing to get Angie on the roster for the celebratory jazz night that upcoming Friday.

"She's an absolutely killer performer," Evan, pretending to be Elijah, spoke over the phone that evening. "She's played piano in about twenty-five ensembles across the United States and Canada."

"Such a liar," Angie hissed, shaking her head.

"Come on, Ang. Not all of what he said is a lie," Luke whispered. "He's just embellishing the story. That's what rich people do to get by."

"I think I'm starting to understand." Angie returned, her voice simmering with sarcasm.

"I'll need her to perform around nine, nine-thirty," Evan continued, ordering the poor employee at The Minty Green around with ease. "Yes, she'll be performing by herself."

When Evan finalized the mission, he smacked his hand across his thigh as the rest of the Keating-Harvey clan howled with excitement.

"Ugh. I can hardly wait till Friday." Heather said.

"I'm terrified," Brittany added.

"Brad's coming, isn't he?" Heather asked.

"Oh yeah. For sure," Brittany said. "Plus, he's bringing the equipment. We're having Angie wear a wire."

"I'm going to mess it up. I'm going to mess it all up." Angie furrowed her brow anxiously. "I'll accidentally flush the wire down the toilet or something."

Brittany laughed good-naturedly. "Angie! You're going to be amazing. Seriously."

"Tomorrow, we go shopping," Heather offered excitedly. "Brittany, you in?"

"Me? I don't really need anything."

Heather rolled her eyes, faking exasperation. "You're telling me you don't want to look absolutely drop-dead gorgeous when you storm into The Minty Green to accuse your ex-husband of stealing ninety-thousand-dollars of revenue out from under you?"

Brittany felt an initially subtle smile stretch from ear to ear.

"There she is," Heather teased. "I have a feeling we're going on a shopping extravaganza tomorrow afternoon. Plus, it's supposed to be kind of warm Friday night. Time to reveal those beautiful legs after a long, cold winter."

* * *

The following afternoon, Heather, Brittany, and Angie met at a downtown Bar Harbor boutique, where a salesgirl hand-selected gorgeous hand-stitched cocktail dresses for the three of them to try on. A stereo in the corner spat out fun tunes from their high school days, and the three girls sang and danced in various stages of undress, feeling giddy.

Brittany was high off the power of the potential of finally, finally showing Conner Radley what she was made of.

"What about this?" The sales girl dangled a black cocktail dress before her, one with a high cinched waist and a flowing taffeta skirt that filtered off below the knee.

Brittany puffed out her cheeks, genuinely impressed. "I can't remember the last time I wore something like this."

The sales girl tilted her head, contemplating the design. "What did you say you need the dress for?"

Brittany laughed. "I want to make my ex-husband regret every horrible thing he ever did and said to me."

The sales girl stuck the dress out even further, basically forcing Brittany to accept it.

"This dress is basically screaming what you just said," the girl told her. "Just try it on. You'll see."

Alone in the dressing room, Brittany attempted to zip the zipper all the way to the space between her shoulder blades but couldn't quite reach it. Outside, Angie and Heather discussed the gown Heather had opted for, which Heather called a "borderline prom dress." Brittany stepped out to ask for assistance, where she found both girls eying her with awe.

"Brittany. Holy, mother, you're a knock-out," Heather told her, clutching the top of her taffeta pink prom-ish dress. "You're..."

"Going to make him regret everything. That's for sure," Angie finished Heather's sentence. "Gosh. You're giving me ideas about what to do to get back at my ex for cheating on me with our bass player."

"Absolute scoundrel," Brittany howled. "Can you help zip me the rest of the way? I want to get a full picture."

Angie hurried over, her own dress ruffling around her knees as she zipped Brittany and patted the soft skin of her upper back. Brittany turned toward the floor-length mirror, her hands on her hips as she took in the full splendor of who she was these days— at forty-six, single, and hunting down Conner for revenge.

Heather smashed her fist onto her palm and said, "First stop, get back at Conner. Next stop... Angie, what's your ex-husband's name again?"

"Felix..." Angie replied, sounding regretful.

"Felix? Ugh. He sounds like the worst," Brittany said. "Like one of those overly-artistic guys who think they're better than everyone else."

"Uh, yeah. You got that right," Angie affirmed.

"What kind of scheme should we come up with to get revenge?" Heather asked. Excitement bubbled in her voice. "Maybe we could make up some kind of feminist group to get back at womens ex-husbands. Women could hire us to create these scenarios."

"It sounds like the plot of a movie," the sales girl chimed in excitedly, clearly enamored with the bubbling friendship between her three customers. "A movie I'd pay good money to go see."

"Maybe I'll write that in my next book," Heather added mischievously. "But what do we call it?"

"The Revenge of the Divorcées," Brittany tried.

"Dramatic, Britt. I almost like it," Heather said.

"What about... Good Riddance?" Angie tried.

"Huh. That has a pretty good ring to it," Heather agreed. "I'll need to pick your ladies' brains for the plot of the book. You'll be noted as having expert opinions."

About forty-five minutes later, Brittany, Angie, and Heather had selected their cocktail dresses for Friday's adventure. Heather paid, waving a hand when Brittany attempted to hand her card over.

"You shouldn't have done that," Brittany said graciously outside the little boutique.

"Don't even start," Heather replied as she slid a large pair of Chanel sunglasses across her nose.

Brittany was grateful for it, but still stewed in sorrow about her own predicament. If Conner hadn't stolen from her... if she'd only had her insurance in place... "silly" purchases like cocktail dresses wouldn't have been such a big deal. All in all, this was a part of life, one she would deal with like all the rest.

The three of them grabbed drinks at a little wine bar near the boutique, giggling about Friday night's upcoming scheme. Brittany felt light as air.

"I'm headed home to keep practicing," Angie told the other ladies a little bit later, splaying a ten-dollar bill on the table before Heather could insist otherwise. "Hannah's going to listen to my entire set tonight and tell me where the kinks are. I have to be perfect."

"Thank you, Angie." Brittany said, taking Angie's hand and squeezing it gently. "I don't know what I would do without you."

Angie gave them both a light shrug. Her right cheek twitched twice as she added, "I don't know what I would have done if you Keating-Harvey people hadn't taken me in as one of your own. I don't know if I'll ever be able to repay you. Hopefully, this is a start."

Chapter Twenty

The plan went like this.

As Angie was one of the performers for jazz night at The Minty Green, she drove herself to Portland on Friday afternoon, several hours before the others' departure. When she arrived, she sent a text message from inside the bar itself.

ANGIE: I'm in!

ANGIE: They're treating me like royalty, kind of.

ANGIE: I think it's because their "big spender Elijah Snow" is the one who set me up with the gig. Wish me luck!

Heather read the texts aloud as Brittany, Brad, Evan, Heather, and Nicole gathered in the living room of the Keating House, nervously killing time. Brad sat on the couch next to Brittany in civilian clothing, a pair of soft, well-worn jeans and a button-down shirt with a subtle yet lovely pattern. This close to him, Brittany noticed the density of his scent, a textured oaky musk that made her skin tingle. *Was this a new purchase?*

Was Brad as nervous as they were about the night ahead, despite his police background? Why did Brittany have the sudden urge to reach out and extend her palm over his?

Shove this thought out of your head.

You have so many other things to worry about.

Brittany realized, with a funny jolt in her stomach, that the voice she used to reprimand herself was incredibly similar to Conner's voice. It was as though her brain had "invented" it to make her feel extra-bad at will— what a pleasurable thing.

"I'll have two officers standing by outside the speakeasy," Brad informed them now. "I explained the situation to the chief of police, who agrees that this has been, in fact, quite fishy behavior, at least when it comes to Elijah Snow and the tracker that was discovered in the wardrobe."

Nicole nodded firmly, lacing her fingers through Evan's. "I don't know if I can thank you enough for the time you've put into this, Brad. Going with Brittany to the auction... Making so many phone calls and interviews..."

"Ultimately, it's been a team effort," Brad affirmed. "With Evan Snow ultimately taking the lead." He cleared his throat, then added, "I'm sure it wasn't an easy thing, suspecting your brother of all this and going with your gut."

"Elijah knows he's living on stolen time," Evan muttered. "It's high time we put a stop to it."

Nicole suggested they order pizza to get their strength up for the night ahead. Abby hustled downstairs at the mention of "pizza" and dialed their favorite place, Rosalie's Pizza, over on Cottage Street. Brad opted to go out and pick it up, as he said he had a rule against getting food delivered.

"I just feel bad for them out there, driving around delivering food to my lazy bones," Brad admitted as he slipped on his jean jacket, making eye contact with Brittany.

Brittany's heart seized with a sudden moment of longing. *Brad was a good man, wasn't he?* This was still more proof of it.

It was decided that they take Brittany's SUV for the night ahead, as it had the space required for all who could make it to Portland. Brittany tossed Brad the keys, grateful he'd been open to driving, as her legs quivered when she was this nervous. She wasn't sure she could quiet them down enough to press the pedals.

Nicole, Evan, and Heather piled in the back, looking like teenagers ready for a night on the town. They squawked about what music they wanted to hear for the drive over, complaining about "today's music and how awful it was" and suggesting that they grab some snacks for what they now called "the stakeout."

As they drew closer to The Minty Green, the mood shifted. It was as though someone had flipped the switch, reminding them that, in actuality, what they were about to do was border-line reckless, like something straight out of a movie. The only problem was: they weren't actually scriptwriters or actors or directors. They were all living this life in real-time, and anything could go wrong at any time.

"It's not like they can do anything," Brittany finally pointed out, mostly to calm her own fears. "It's a public place. Angie's one of the jazz performers. She'll be protected."

"And I guess the worst thing that could happen is that we don't get the information we need," Heather added, her voice wavering.

"Which is not the end of the world," Brittany reminded them. "Yes, I'm out a lot of money. But I'm a survivor. I'll figure something out."

"And we'll help you do it," Heather piped up. "You're not alone in this, Brittany. No matter how proud you like to believe you are."

When they parked in the nearest parking lot to the speakeasy, it was ten past eight-thirty. Angie was slated to perform at nine-sharp. They sat in silence as Brad set up the recording device and the speaker, which would pick up the wire that Angie had attached to her. Brittany sent Angie a text to say they were ready to go when she was, and a moment later, the speaker ruffled and spat with the sounds of inner workings of The Minty Green.

There: the beautiful yip of a trumpet, the clink of a piano, the soulful sound of the E-flat saxophone. Brittany leaned her head against the headrest and closed her eyes, trying to imagine the interior of the bar itself, of Angie in the gorgeous dress she'd just purchased, hovering off to the side, alone. Perhaps Elijah and Conner were seated at a two-top, listening to the music and drinking expensive cocktails one after another. Conner had adored the way Elijah threw his wealth around. She'd imagined that lately, with Elijah at his side, Conner had had the time of his life.

Brittany prayed that time was over. The likes of Conner Radley didn't deserve such goodness in his life. He didn't deserve thirty-five-dollar cocktails in exclusive clubs or flirtations with beautiful women in cocktail dresses or drives home in Ferraris and Lamborghinis. If it was up to her, he deserved jail time.

It was a hard thing for the mother of his children to wrap her mind around. Perhaps this was a sign of her own internal growth. Perhaps this was proof that she'd finally gotten rid of his hold on her.

"Hey, guys." Angie's voice rang through the speaker. "I stepped into the bathroom really quick. You can hear everything all right?"

"Loud and clear, Ang," Brittany said into Brad's microphone. "How's it going there?"

"Well... The guys are here. I can tell you that much," Angie muttered. "And they've already racked up a pretty significant tab."

"Sounds like our boys," Evan offered sarcastically.

"Have you had any contact with them?" Brad asked.

"Nothing so far," Angie said. "But I want to wait until after my performance. I'm shivering with nerves. It isn't like me. I've performed upwards of ten thousand times."

"I'm sure that's not even a gross exaggeration," Brittany told her.

"But immediately after I step away from the piano, I'll put your plan into action," Angie continued. "I promise you that. I'm not afraid of those rich jerks just because they're throwing money around. I'm used to that back in Chicago. People think they're stronger just because they have a bank account to fall back on. I can see right through it."

Brittany sat in stunned silence as Angie cut off the conversation and headed back to the speakeasy. Brad reached across the SUV and gripped her elbow tenderly, drawing her eyes toward his.

Through the speaker, the MC of the night's jazz performance announced Angie Montague, a jazz pianist from Chicago, Illinois.

"But she's just moved to Bar Harbor, folks," the MC continued as Angie marched closer to the sound. "And she's told me in secret that she's here to stay."

He paused for a moment. There was the sound of Angie assembling herself in front of the piano. Brittany's stomach twisted into knots. She wasn't sure what she was currently nervous about— was it the operation they'd planned or empathetic stage fright?

"Here she is. Take it away, Angie Montague," the MC cried out to the audience.

The speakeasy audience applauded, tossing out whistles as Angie struck her first few chords of a classic jazz favorite, "Sing, Sing, Sing," before she suddenly whirled into an improvisation all on her own. In the SUV, the listeners were captivated, in thrall of her musicality and her ease on the keys.

When she finished this first tune, Evan whistled low and

said, "Yeah. She was the perfect person to send in there tonight."

"Why do you say that?" Nicole asked.

"Because Elijah won't want to be seen with anyone else but her. She's something special."

Angie's set was meant to last twenty-five minutes. She breezed through her set-list with a powerful force, captivating the audience so much that there was very little conversation throughout the speakeasy. When she struck the final chord, the crowd erupted into applause and robust whistles. Someone shouted, "Encore!" which brought on another round of "encore, encore!" Angie rounded out her set with a final rendition of Queen's "Somebody to Love," which she'd jazzified. Throughout the audience, everyone sang the words they knew joyously, overwhelmed that she'd connected the jazz world with this other rock one.

"That's Angie Montague, everyone," the MC announced, genuinely aghast. "She tells me she plays most nights at the Keating Inn over in Bar Harbor. I think this might mean I'll be taking a trip over there pretty dang soon."

There next came the sounds of revelers wanting to wrap themselves around Angie. They asked her where she'd learned to play like that and whether she accepted private party jobs and if she'd considered putting together a record. Angie seemed overwhelmed with the intensity of everyone's questions.

And then, out of the blue, came the sound of Elijah Snow's voice.

"Angie! Let's get you out of this chaos. You like whiskey?"

Angie stuttered her answer nervously. "Um. Yes? Yes. I like whiskey."

"Great. Everyone, give the musician some space. She just performed for thirty minutes. Isn't that enough for you?" Elijah guffawed.

"It's showtime," Evan breathed in the back of the SUV.

"I'm so nervous." Heather whispered.

"Shh..." Nicole pressed her finger against her lips, a classic older sister move.

"Thank you for getting me out of there," Angie told Elijah. "I thought I was going to pass out."

"Don't mention it. When he said you lived in Bar Harbor, I already knew I had to talk to you. I was born and raised in Bar Harbor myself. Such a fine place. I don't get there as much as I used to, but now that you're a resident, I'll have to make a few more pit-stops. Plus, I own a number of restaurants and bars in Bar Harbor. We're always looking for talent such as yourself."

"Oh, that would be so lovely," Angie breathed.

"If you don't mind me asking, why do you play so often at the Keating Inn?" Elijah asked. "I used to own the property that way but recently sold it."

"What a liar," Evan coughed.

"Oh, I stumbled in one day and started playing the piano. The front desk manager asked if I might want to perform a few nights a week. I was hungry for work, so I accepted," Angie explained.

"She's such a little actress!" Heather cried.

Again, Nicole shushed her as Brittany leaned toward the speaker, expectant.

"Didn't I tell you I'd go ask her to sit with us?" Elijah said proudly. "I always get what I want."

"Excuse him. He's been gifted with admittedly too much confidence."

This was Conner Radley's voice. Conner Radley, the man Brittany had loved and lost— the man she'd had children with, balanced the check book with, fought with, and ached for. She would have recognized his voice out of a million other voices. And now, he spoke to Angie flirtatiously, as though he actually wanted to date her.

Was this jealousy Brittany felt? She tried to shove it out of her mind and focus on the task at hand.

"You love my confidence," Elijah said boastfully. "Angie, this is my dear friend, Conner Radley. And Conner, this, as you might know, is Angie. She's new to Bar Harbor."

"Pleased to make your acquaintance," Conner told her. "I recently left Bar Harbor myself."

"Did you? Why did you leave?" Angie asked innocently.

"Ah. Well. Isn't that a story?" Conner asked. Then, he and Elijah burst into horrible laughter.

Brittany's stomach twisted strangely. Elijah then hailed a passing waiter, who took his order of three Manhattans. It seemed so like Elijah Snow not to care if a Manhattan was Angie's drink or not. He seemed the kind of guy who wanted to control every little portion of the evening, down to who drank what, which table to sit at, and what time to leave.

"I guess that's life, isn't it?" Angie finally said, her voice wavering slightly. "One story after another. Some of them are messier than others. And others are nightmares."

"She gets it," Elijah cried. "What about you, our beautiful pianist? Care to share one or two of those stories you have up your sleeves?"

"I don't know if I'm the type of girl to show all my cards like that," Angie returned. "Not without making some kind of trade."

"The lady likes to play," Elijah offered as Conner cackled.

"I appreciate strength in a woman," Conner told her.

Brittany had the sudden urge to scream but kept it trapped tight in her throat. This was the ultimate test of her courage and her confidence and her sense of self. Had she truly grown out of Conner Radley's latches? Or was the fact that she now hung on his every word in a nearby SUV proof that she hadn't— not in the least?

Chapter Twenty-One

"Here you are, Mr. Snow." The waiter arrived with their drinks. There was the clunk, clunk, clunk of each drink's placement on the table. Brittany could envision them: Angie in her beautiful cocktail dress, Conner in a suit she'd probably picked out for him, and Elijah in some Italian-bought garb that cost upward of five-thousand dollars. To anyone else, it probably seemed that the biggest high-rollers of the night had "captured" the promising and gorgeous pianist. How lucky she was. She'd get free drinks the rest of the night.

"Let's make a toast," Elijah instructed. "To surprise encounters and wild, wild nights ahead."

Conner, Angie, and Elijah clinked their glasses together. Brittany's heart cracked with fear. Elijah had clear control over the conversation. How then, would Angie manipulate the situation to get the information they needed?

Suddenly, there came the sound of the other police officers, who sat listening in a vehicle across the parking lot.

"Officer Wethers? You there? Over."

160

"We're here, over." Brad's eyes shifted back and forth, proof of his frustration.

"We're wondering where she's going with this or if she plans to just drink and gossip with them all night. Over." The other police officers apparently had better plans for the evening.

Brad rolled his eyes into the back of his head. "She can't very well just demand the information the minute she sits down with them. Over."

Annoyed, the other cops didn't respond. Heather groaned inwardly in the back seat, muttering, "I don't know what they think spying is. According to everything I know about it, it's supposed to be as boring as hell."

"That's why I brought snacks." Nicole reached into her backpack and dragged out a big box of cookies, which she passed out to everyone else. "I added extra butter, so there's no crunch. We can listen to their conversation better that way."

"Good thinking," Heather mumbled, her mouth filled with chocolatey cookie goodness.

Through the speaker, Elijah spoke now about his apparent fascination with jazz music, that it was never the same moment-for-moment, that it seemed as organic as trees or clouds or water or life itself. Angie agreed with him whole-heartedly, saying, "Gosh, it's so wonderful to meet someone who really gets that about jazz music. I was married for many years to a jazz musician, and I don't think even he fully grasped what you've just told me."

Elijah was clearly pleased with the compliment. "Uh oh. There she goes, telling us a secret from her past. Conner, what do you think about that?"

"I think whoever this ex is, he messed up big, letting you go," Conner countered.

"Messed up big indeed," Elijah affirmed. "You have to tell

us what happened. Why you two aren't together anymore, making jazz music as the sun sets over the ocean somewhere."

"Well, it's a pretty long story. I'll need one from each of you in return." Angie replied playfully.

"Depends how good the story is," Elijah quipped.

"Yeah. Let's hear it," Conner goaded her.

Angie buzzed her lips, then began. "Well. We started our own jazz ensemble together—a really prosperous thing in Chicago. We played two or three nights a week, which is a Godsend in the music industry. I thought we had everything we ever dreamed of. But then, one day, I learned that actually, he was having an affair with our bass player. And in one fell swoop, I was kicked out of our jazz band and out of our marriage."

Elijah and Conner were impressed.

"That's horrific," Elijah muttered. "You lost your livelihood and your love all at once."

"You're telling me," Angie affirmed. "And then a few weeks later, my dad died. Then I found out that actually, he was my adopted dad. But that's a whole other story."

"Jesus! She's got all the stories, Conner. I'm feeling slightly competitive. I don't know about you," Elijah said.

"Slightly..." Conner's voice was sharp and strange. "Although having someone use and abuse you seems pretty par for the course when it comes to marriage. Elijah, you wouldn't know. You never bothered with it."

"And I thank my lucky stars every single day," Elijah replied with a wicked laugh.

Brittany's stomach curdled with a mix of fear and anger. Seeming to sense this, Brad again reached across the SUV and gripped her hand, lacing his fingers through hers. He was her rock.

"Oh, I love divorce stories." Angie said mischievously. "Tell me what happened?"

"Well, there I was, minding my own business in Boston when this girl comes up to me. She really knocks my socks off, you know. She seems to love me to pieces. When she asks me to move to Bar Harbor with her, I barely hesitate. And I'm a fifth-generation Bostonian."

"Wow..." Angie sounded impressed.

"But over the years, something in her changed. She became abusive in a really backward way, wherein she would basically invent terrible things I'd done to her and throw them in my face. Around Bar Harbor, people wouldn't stop talking about what a monster I was. I started to feel like I actually was a monster, or at least an alien. The only friend I truly had was Elijah."

"I kept telling him to get out of it," Elijah chimed in.

"Liars," Brittany muttered. "Such liars."

"That sounds so manipulative," Angie said empathetically. "I can't imagine."

"You really can't," Conner affirmed, sounding arrogant as ever. "And you have to believe me, Angie. I fought to make that marriage work. I fought tooth and nail, just like you did because I loved her. And then, one day, she told me that if I didn't leave the house that moment, she would call the cops and tell them I'd beat her up. She had a baseball bat lifted like she planned to whack herself in the face."

"You're kidding," Angie whispered.

"I wish I was," Conner continued.

"What a monster," Angie agreed.

"She's good at playing along," Heather added in the back of the SUV. "I would probably have punched him in the face by now."

Nicole shushed her again.

"But you've figured a way to pay her back," Elijah added.

Conner howled with laughter as Angie stuttered with confusion.

"What are you talking about? Pay her back? Pay her back for all the pain she caused you?" Angie asked.

"Come on, Elijah. We don't need to talk about everything." Conner told him.

"You're right. It's still early for those kinds of talks." Elijah agreed.

"You're killing me, guys," Angie whined. "I told you so much about my past."

"Not about your surprise adoption," Elijah pointed out. "Or what brought you to Bar Harbor in the first place."

"It's literally only nine-forty-five," Conner told them pointedly. "Drink your drink, Ang. Me and Elijah need you to keep up with us."

Everyone in the SUV let out a sigh of sorrow. Clearly, it would be a long night. Brittany grabbed another cookie from Nicole's box and chewed gingerly at the sides, frustrated. Bit-by-bit, Elijah, Conner, and Angie's conversations swept over other areas, about Elijah's other favorite bars in the area, about Conner's new idea for a business that sold space for pop-up restaurants in the Portland area, and about Elijah's insistence that he didn't actually have a kid in the Florida Keys, even though some woman kept contacting him and demanding child support.

"Wow. I didn't know about that," Evan spoke for the first time in a while. "That's dramatic."

"Do you think he's just trying to show off? Making up a story?" Nicole asked.

"I think that was his honest voice," Evan said. "But yeah. It's difficult to tell."

Suddenly, there came the sound of the other police officer's voice from the car opposite them in the parking lot.

"Wethers? We might pack it in. We don't see this as anything more than a waste of time. Over."

Brad again rolled his eyes. "We need to be patient. She's playing them both like a fiddle."

"We'll give it thirty more minutes tops," the other cop said, disgruntled. "Then we're headed to our hotel room for the night."

Around twenty minutes later, Angie finally asked, "It seems like you two are experts at all relationship stuff."

"Experts? I don't know about that. We know our way around women. That's for sure," Elijah confessed. "Conner especially. Although that's not something we should say in front of you, is it? Especially since your husband cheated on you."

"I'd never cheat on someone like you," Conner affirmed. "You're so sweet, Angie. So caring. I can tell that you'd give your all to your marriage. It's a beautiful thing."

Inwardly, Brittany seethed with anger, blinking back tears. Brad's fingers wrapped tighter around her hand. Conner had manipulated her and made her feel powerless and small. Now, he admitted he'd cheated on her, as well. It was like the insults just kept coming.

"Don't worry yourself," Angie told Conner. "I understand that not all relationships are perfect. Not everyone is meant to be together forever. And besides, based on what you said, your ex-wife had it coming." She cleared her throat, then added, "By the way. You'd mentioned you were in the midst of getting even with her. How do you two think I should get back at my husband for what he did?"

Elijah roared with laughter. *How many drinks had they had thus far?* Brittany had lost count. Probably this was better, drawing them deeper into their drunken stupor and making their tongues looser.

"We gotta tell her," Elijah said smoothly. "Come on. It's a great story."

"I don't know..." Conner was doubtful.

"Seriously. Who is she going to tell?" Elijah demanded.

"Yeah, Conner. Who am I going to tell?" Angie asked, a smile playing out through her voice.

"All right. Dammit. If you're going to twist my arm." Conner paused, took a sip of his drink, cleared his throat, and then said, "I had some insider intel about her insurance provider. I knew she hadn't done due diligence around some of the property she owned. And let's just say I made upward of one hundred thousand dollars of inventory disappear."

Brittany erupted from her seat in the SUV. Her skin felt like it was on fire. With the SUV door open, she leaped into the chill of the April evening. Inside the SUV, the others sat in stunned silence as Conner continued to confess to even more— that he profited off of the items he'd stolen, that he didn't regret it, that he hoped and prayed every day that his ex-wife was miserable and crying herself to sleep at night.

"It's what she deserves," Conner spat, his tone harsh. His demeanor didn't have a care in the world. "For what she put me through, she should rot in her sorrows forever."

"Well said," Elijah cried.

"Absolutely. Well said," Angie agreed.

There was the clink of their whiskey glasses. Across the parking lot, the two police officers sprung out of their cop car and headed toward the secret entrance to the speakeasy, which Angie had told them was located on the other side of the butcher shop.

"Brittany, we need to stay here while they arrest him!" Brad called from within the SUV.

But Brittany had gone through too much to wait around for something to happen. Spontaneously, she rushed forward, hustling after the other cops. Brad leaped out of the SUV and bounded after her, while Evan, Heather, and Nicole jumped out, as well.

Now that they couldn't hear what went on between Angie,

Elijah, and Conner any longer, Brittany felt like she was deep underwater, with only her thoughts to keep her company.

Conner had cheated on her.

He'd manipulated her.

For twenty-five years, he'd made her feel about two inches tall.

And now, he'd stolen ninety-thousand dollars worth of inventory and bragged about it to the first pretty face who'd come along.

What an idiot she was for having loved him.

How could she ever forgive herself?

Chapter Twenty-Two

Brittany burst into the speakeasy with the intensity of a sprinter at an Olympic race. On either side of the front door, people gathered and gawked, their jaws hanging open as they took in sight of two in-uniform police officers as they stood before the table of Conner, Elijah, and Angie. Angie remained at the table, still playing dumb, her lips wrapped around the tiny straw of her Manhattan drink. Elijah chewed the inside of his cheek nervously.

"What the hell?" A well-dressed man near the front door caught sight of Brittany, who probably looked like a crazy stalker. Her cheeks were chilly; all the blood had drained to her feet.

"It's always so weird here after a certain time," another onlooker muttered. "We should hit the road. Can you call an Uber?"

"No. My friend here doesn't have to go anywhere with you. You have absolutely no evidence that he did anything wrong." Elijah leaped up from his stool, wagging a finger toward the police officers.

"What makes you think we're not going to arrest you as well, Mr. Snow?" one of the cops threatened in the politest way possible. Enough to make him squirm in his seat.

The corners of Elijah's smile curved toward the ground dramatically. Conner's lips parted with surprise. With Elijah by his side, Conner was accustomed to getting away with every-thing— even, probably, murder if he'd tried it.

Suddenly, a cop stepped around Conner and latched hand-cuffs around his wrist. Conner wailed out over the music from the speaker system, his eyes glowing with pain and surprise. His upper body smacked the table, and the sound was proof enough that it was painful. His eyes then lifted toward the front door of the speakeasy, where Brittany stood with her arms hanging slack at her sides.

The look Conner gave her at that moment was one she would never forget, not as long as she lived.

The look told her everything she needed to know.

It told her that Conner Radley was incapable of love in any capacity.

It told her that he hated her to her core— that maybe his hatred for her had grown steadily over the years, especially as her confidence and her business had grown.

It also told her that he knew she'd gotten the better of him. He didn't know how. And maybe he never would.

"Come on." The cop tugged Conner toward the front door just as Brad burst in, gasping for air. He stalled beside Brittany, wrapping an arm around her waist tenderly as Conner and the cop passed by.

Brittany was petrified as Conner and the cop stepped only two feet away from her. Her entire body shivered with sorrow and fear. But when he got close, Conner whispered something she would never have expected.

"Brittany. Why would you do this? Don't you know how much I love you?"

The words rattled through her. For a horrible split-second, Brittany half-believed them. She half-wanted to tell the cops to call off the operation, to make peace.

But a split-second after that, Brittany remembered herself. She remembered all she'd been through. And she lifted her chin to say, "Conner. I know, beyond a shadow of a doubt, that you never knew what love was. Not the day we met, not the day we married, not the day our children were born, and not now. I feel bad for you. But at the same time, I hope I never have to lay eyes on you again."

"Come on! No more theatrics," the cop cried, tugging a deflated Conner back down the staircase. Another cop appeared directly behind the other, bringing Elijah along with him. Elijah looked at a loss, like a little boy who'd just been told it was bedtime "or else."

When they disappeared down the dark shadows of the staircase, Brittany turned back toward the shocked faces of the rest of the bar. They took her and Brad in, flabbergasted, then returned their attention to their drinks. Slowly, someone lifted the volume of the speaker system once more. Gossip bubbled around them. "What the hell just happened?" everyone demanded of everyone else.

Angie hustled up from her circular table, her eyes wide with shock. "I cannot believe that worked!" She flung her arms around Brittany just as Evan, Nicole, and Heather stepped into the speakeasy to join them in a group hug. They held one another in the walkway there by the entrance, blocking everyone else and forgetting to care.

"Angie. You were so brilliant tonight," Brittany breathed, stepping back as her eyes filled with tears. As she swiped them away, she forced herself to say all she needed to say. "And the rest of you were so incredible to come tonight. It was truly one of the most spectacular nights of my life. I don't know what I would have done without you."

As Evan rushed up to grab them all a round of celebratory drinks, a man in a suit and tie approached suddenly, his eyes alight with excitement. He turned toward Angie, cocked his head, and said, "Hey, I heard you play earlier. You were just fantastic. We really need more performers in the Portland area if you're willing to make the drive. The pay is better than most." He passed her his business card and offered a gentle smile.

As he walked away from the rest of them, Angie waved the card excitedly, making eye contact with Brittany. "Tonight, might have changed my life."

"No reason you can't take up work in the spy industry as well," Nicole suggested with a laugh. "Maybe they're hiring at the CIA?"

Angie laughed good-naturedly. "Do you think they'll always let me wear a cocktail dress like this?"

"They'd better," Heather affirmed. "You look like a knockout."

A little more than an hour later, Evan, Nicole, and Heather sat upright passed out in the back seat of Brittany's SUV while a sober Brad guided them gently toward Bar Harbor, toward home. Brittany was amazed at the silence of the night, at the resolution in her heart, at the ease with which she took Brad's hand and held it lovingly, wanting no other touch but his.

In a way, she felt bad for Conner, felt bad that her children would have to decide whether or not they wanted to visit him in prison, and that he'd spend most of his life in a six by eight cell eating the same old bland food over and over again. In another way, she was so grateful for the freedom she now felt, and the assurance that soon, she would have her inventory back. Soon, her dream would become a reality once again.

"Thank you for all you've done for me, Brad," Brittany breathed, not loud enough for the others in back to awaken.

"The past few weeks have truly changed my life. And I wouldn't take them back for anything."

Brad cleared his throat as a look of sorrow passed over his face. Brittany squeezed his hand just the tiniest bit harder.

"I feel the same way," Brad told her, his voice only a whisper.

Again, Brittany allowed silence to pass between them. How could she possibly describe the hope she felt for their future? How could she tell him that already, she'd envisioned Brad at the house she shared with Valerie, perhaps changing paint colors on the walls and reassembling furniture? How could she describe to him the density of her dreams?

Instead, she just said, "I know you've had love before, Brad. I know you've had real love, the kind that sticks to your bones and makes you feel bigger and better than you ever were before. But I haven't had that. I don't even know how to build it. If you feel up to it... If you really want to... I'd love to make something like that with you. It'll be a journey, one with many ups and downs and in-betweens. But I'm ready to try."

The highway at night was dense with springtime fog. Their headlights beamed out through it, illustrating only the shadows of the surrounding vehicles. The ever-responsible Brad drove a steady sixty-five miles per hour without even using the Cruise Control. And over the next seconds, Brittany half-prayed he wouldn't answer her, as it would allow them to live in this in-between forever, both knowing and not-knowing at once.

Finally, Brad cleared his throat.

"One of the biggest gifts of my life was learning how to love," he told her, his voice textured and deep. "And they tell you that all loves are different. That they show you different things about yourself. That they give you so many different stories and dreams."

Brittany's eyes welled with tears. She dropped her head

against the headrest as they careened through the impossibility of this dark and scary night.

"It would be my privilege and my honor to know you," Brad offered. "But I suppose we have to start with square one, don't we?"

Brittany furrowed her brow. "What do you mean? Square one?"

The corners of Brad's lips curved upward, proof of his playful smile.

"I reckon I have to take you out on a proper first date."

Brittany nearly collapsed with giggles. Her laughter rolled out across the highway and tickled Heather, Nicole, and Evan's tired ears.

"A proper date, huh?" Brittany echoed gently, careful to quiet herself down.

"I've lost my touch when it comes to dating," Brad told her. "But I have a hunch we'll be okay."

Brittany marveled at the beauty of such a simple sentence. As the light of the moon flashed out from the fluttering clouds above them, she chose to repeat what he'd said, articulating the syllables firmly.

"You know what? I have a hunch we'll be okay, too."

Coming Next

Coming Next in the Bar Harbor Series

Other Books by Katie

The Vineyard Sunset Series

Secrets of Mackinac Island Series

Sisters of Edgartown Series

A Katama Bay Series

A Mount Desert Island Series

Connect with Katie Winters

Amazon
BookBub
Facebook
Newsletter

To receive exclusive updates from Katie Winters please sign up
to be on her Newsletter!

CPSIA information can be obtained
at www.ICGtesting.com
Printed in the USA
BVHW032307091022
649053BV00012B/227